UNDER THE IRON BRIDGE

A HOLOCAUST REMEMBRANCE
BOOK FOR YOUNG READERS

UNDER THE IRON BRIDGE

KATHY KACER

Second Story Press

Library and Archives Canada Cataloguing in Publication

Title: Under the iron bridge / Kathy Kacer.
Names: Kacer, Kathy, 1954- author.
Series: Holocaust remembrance book for young readers.
Description: Series statement: A Holocaust remembrance book for
  young readers
Identifiers: Canadiana (print) 2021013593X | Canadiana (ebook)
  20210136073 | ISBN 9781772602050 (softcover) |
  ISBN 9781772602067 (EPUB)
Classification: LCC PS8571.A33 U53 2021 | DDC jC813/.54—dc23

Edited by Sarah Swartz

Cover photo: iStock.com/Alex Muslovets
Photo on page 216: World History Archive / Alamy Stock Photo
Photo on page 218: Sueddeutsche Zeitung Photo / Alamy Stock Photo

Printed and bound in Canada

*Second Story Press gratefully acknowledges the support of the Ontario Arts
Council and the Canada Council for the Arts for our publishing program.
We acknowledge the financial support of the Government of Canada through
the Canada Book Fund.*

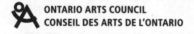

ONTARIO ARTS COUNCIL
CONSEIL DES ARTS DE L'ONTARIO

Canada Council   Conseil des Arts
for the Arts   du Canada

Funded by the Government of Canada
Financé par le gouvernement du Canada

Canadä

Published by
SECOND STORY PRESS
20 Maud Street, Suite 401
Toronto, ON M5V 2M5
www.secondstorypress.ca

MIX
Paper from
responsible sources
FSC
www.fsc.org   FSC® C016245

For my best buddy, Rose—my friend for life

Our song is freedom, love and life,
We're the Pirates of the Edelweiss.[1]

[1] A song from the Edelweiss Pirates. "The German Teens Who Sang and Danced Their Nazi Resistance" by Abby Sher, Jewish Telegraphic Agency, *Jewniverse*, 2016.

PROLOGUE

Wednesday, November 9, 1938

The flame was visible in the cold night sky, even before Paul and the other members of the Hitler Youth had rounded the corner and approached the building. Up ahead was the New Synagogue of Düsseldorf, which most of the Jewish families of the city attended. Tonight, it was unrecognizable. Hot embers leapt and danced in the air. Ribbons of fire illuminated the sky. And the smell! Thick and noxious, it filled Paul's lungs, choking him. He coughed and doubled over as if he'd been punched in the stomach.

When he lifted his head, he could see Nazi soldiers flinging torches at the building, tossing them inside the door and high onto the roof to stoke the fire. German police stood by and did nothing to stop them.

Franz, the leader of the Hitler Youth group, came to stand next to him and the other boys. "This is how we treat the Jews!" he shouted above the noise of blistering wood and hissing flames. "Destroy their synagogues and burn them to the ground."

Paul's heart beat wildly as his eyes frantically roamed the crowd. Where were the Edelweiss Pirates? Where were his fellow freedom-fighters, rebels who were trying to battle against this kind of senseless action?

"Find some rocks!" Franz ordered. "The bigger the better. Throw them at the windows and listen to the shattering glass."

To demonstrate, Franz searched the ground and found a rock that was sharp and jagged. Then, he turned toward the building and threw it into a window. Glass shards, fueled by the fire, exploded into the air and rained down on the sidewalk, already littered with glass, metal, and wood.

This was the cue needed to unleash the other boys in the Hitler Youth group. With a whoop that echoed above the sound of the fire, they scattered, finding their own rocks and throwing them at the synagogue building.

Paul was too stunned to move. His feet seemed glued to the ground. He wanted to run away as fast and as far as he could. This was not what he thought would happen. It was never what he had planned, not since he had been forced to join the Hitler Youth months earlier. Paul's best friend, Harold, standing next to him, seemed equally paralyzed.

"I don't want to do this," Harold whispered.

"I'm not going to listen to them," Paul replied, as much to himself as to Harold. "I don't care what happens."

Franz was by their side in a second. "What's wrong with the two of you?" he demanded. "Didn't you hear my order? Find a rock and throw it!"

Dazed, Harold sank down to his knees in search of something to throw. He finally found a small rock, hardly more than a stone. Under Franz's hard stare, Harold tossed it toward the building. It didn't go far enough, rolling several feet from the synagogue door.

Franz grabbed Harold by the collar and pulled him up close to his face. But before he could shout more orders, there was another commotion up ahead. A group of people were being marched in front of the burning synagogue, heads down, feet stumbling across the debris. There must have been more than one hundred of them.

Paul knew immediately that they were Jews. They wore the recognizable yellow star on their jackets and sweaters. Several of the men wore skullcaps on their heads. They swayed back and forth as they walked, eyes closed as if in prayer. Women held on to their husbands and children. Elderly couples hugged each other.

Franz, momentarily distracted, released Harold and straightened his jacket. "You are about to witness another great moment." He called out to the boys to come closer. They crowded around him, still clutching their rocks.

Paul couldn't hear a thing. Sounds were muffled in his ears. Franz was shouting something more, but Paul didn't know what. All he could do was stand, mouth open, staring at the group of Jewish people slowly moving forward in front of him. And he couldn't take his eyes off one person in particular.

It was Analia.

CHAPTER 1

Tuesday, August 30, 1938

Three Months Earlier

"I don't understand why you haven't signed up for the Hitler Youth."

Fifteen-year-old Paul Ritter was walking home from school with his good friend, Harold Becker. And as often happened these days, Harold was yammering away at Paul on his favorite subject. "It's an honor to serve Adolf Hitler," Harold insisted, naming the leader of the ruling Nazi government and jabbing Paul lightly in the arm. "The best way to show our devotion to him is to join up."

Paul exhaled a long breath and reached up to run his hand through his blond mop of hair, which threatened to fall into his eyes. His forehead was lined with perspiration in the hot August sun. But it was Harold's constant blabbering that was making him really sweat. The Hitler Youth was the official organization of the Nazi party that brought boys between the ages of fourteen and eighteen together and trained them to eventually become part of the military that served Adolf Hitler. Boys of Paul's age were being pressured to join whether they wanted to or not. And Paul did not!

"I don't know why you're refusing to go," Harold persisted. "Hitler is the greatest leader for Germany."

It was true that Germany under Adolf Hitler was poised to become a superpower. This was 1938, and Hitler had already taken over Austria, claiming it as part of the greater Germany. He had declared that other countries would soon follow. No one doubted him. And here in the city of Düsseldorf, the evidence of Hitler's rule was everywhere. Flags with swastikas, the symbol of the Nazi party, flew from every building. Pictures of Hitler could be seen inside every department store, office building, and school, including in Paul's classroom. The airwaves blasted speeches from Hitler, declaring his strength and the superiority of Germany. At rallies and parades around the city, citizens cheered and sang out "*Heil Hitler,*" hail to Hitler, and "*Sieg Heil,*" hail to victory. Crowds worked themselves into a frenzy faster than a storm brewing on the summer horizon. Paul had seen it all and still he had his doubts.

"Joining the Hitler Youth was the best thing I could have done," Harold insisted. "The meetings are so inspiring. We sing songs that praise our great *Führer*."

Führer, our great leader. That's how everyone referred to Hitler.

"We exercise to make ourselves strong and fit." Harold rolled up his sleeve and flexed a sorry-looking muscle. Paul stifled a laugh. It would take more than a few exercises to build up Harold's body. He was definitely a physical weakling. His strength was in math and sciences. The two had become great friends when Paul had come to Harold for help in math a couple of years earlier. With Harold's help, Paul's grades had soared, and their friendship was sealed. But while Harold could easily calculate sums in his head, he had never been good at sports. Paul, on the other hand, was an athlete, adept at long-distance running and soccer.

"We go on camping trips," Harold continued, oblivious to Paul's reaction. "It's better than any group I've ever belonged to."

Paul snorted. "When I was in the boy scouts, we trained and exercised and camped, and sang songs. There was nothing wrong with that group."

Years earlier, Hitler had banned the boy scouts and all other youth organizations. Now, the Hitler Youth group was the only boys' group in town.

"Trust me, this is so much better," Harold continued.

"We talk about becoming real soldiers and fighting for our country."

"Why do we need to talk about becoming soldiers?" Paul was growing increasingly irritated with his friend. "We're not at war."

"But we could be one day. Everyone says we will be. And we have to be prepared."

Paul leaned his head back and let the sun wash over him. "That's enough, Harold," he finally said. "I don't want to talk about this anymore."

The two walked in silence passing the market on Carlsplatz. The market teemed with shoppers rushing from stall to stall, buying cheese, meat, spices, and vegetables to take home for dinner. The bakery had rows and rows of fresh cakes and cookies on display. Often, Paul and Harold stopped in the market on the way home from school to buy potato pancakes that, when served off the pan, still sizzled from the frying oil. But food was not the only attraction here. There were basket makers, weavers, and leather producers who sang out to customers to stop and sample their products. Walking through the market was an experience in having all one's senses—smell, sight, sound—bombarded, and in the best possible way. Harold glanced at Paul and raised an eyebrow, a cue that he was hungry. But Paul turned away; he was in no mood to stop today.

A streetcar rumbled along Benrather Strasse. The two

boys waited for it to pass before sprinting across the busy street and continuing to walk home. The heat was still strong, even at the end of the day. Paul reached up once more to flip his long hair off his face.

"You know you'd have to get a haircut if you joined up," Harold said, breaking the silence. Harold's hair was just as blond as Paul's, but Harold had recently cropped his short with a sharp, even part on one side. "The Hitler Youth insists that everyone be neat and clean-cut. Is that the reason you don't want to be part of it? You don't want to cut your hair?"

"Can you not take a hint?" Paul declared, coming to a stop and facing his friend, his voice rising. "I don't care about a stupid haircut."

"Then what is it?" Harold pressed him once more.

Paul stared at Harold. "Hitler is trying to control every part of our lives. He's stopping us from being able to think for ourselves. Besides, have you heard what he says about Jewish people?"

This was probably the part that disturbed Paul most of all. He might have gone along with so many other boys and agreed to be part of the Hitler Youth. He could have set aside his concerns about the military training. But he rankled when he heard Hitler ranting about the Jews. He called them poisonous, evil, inferior. There were already rules and laws in Germany, and now in other countries that Hitler controlled, that limited where Jewish people could shop or work. And whenever Hitler denounced Jewish people, which he did in every speech, he hailed the German people as the master race, superior to everyone else.

"Have you heard the disgusting things he says about Jews?" Paul asked again.

Harold eyed him curiously. "Of course, I have. Everyone has. I don't particularly like what he says. But why does it bother you so much?"

"Nobody has the right to treat other people like that!" Paul snapped.

And there it was! It just made no sense to Paul that Hitler could hate one group of people so completely and could convince so many others to hate them as well just because of their religion. That's not how Paul had been raised. His parents despised Hitler and everything he stood for, especially his proclamations about Jews. Mama and Papa had always taught Paul that all life was important and valuable; all people were equal. It was a standpoint that was not popular in Germany these days. In fact, his parents often warned Paul not to be too vocal in his defense of Jewish people. It might get him into trouble. There had been rumors of citizens being arrested if they stood up for their Jewish friends and neighbors. In fact, people were encouraged to turn in anyone who opposed what Hitler stood for. Paul hadn't talked about any of this with Harold, and Harold was his best friend.

But if Harold was disturbed by anything Paul was saying, he didn't show it. The two boys continued walking, silent once more, until they came closer to their homes. Paul and Harold lived in the Unterbilk suburb of Düsseldorf, a quiet community, close to the Rhine River, where small, identical brick houses lined up side by side. The only way to distinguish one from another was by color. One house was painted green, another blue, another yellow. It was as if each house contributed to what looked like a colorful patchwork. Paul's house, a deep blue shade, was on one street, and Harold's, painted bright red, was a block away.

The boys came to a stop at the corner, still quiet, eyeing one another. Paul shuffled his foot against the pavement and shifted his book bag to his other shoulder. The silence between them hung in the air like a low cloud.

"Do you feel like going to the beach on the weekend?" Harold asked weakly. It was his attempt at a peace offering.

Paul paused and then smiled at his friend, grateful that Harold had taken this first step to ease the tension between them. "Sure. That'd be great."

"Look," Harold said before turning away. "I don't want to fight with you about this. But just think about what I've said, okay?"

Anything to get Harold off his back, and anything to

avoid another strained stand-off. "Okay," Paul replied. "I'll think about it."

But before finally parting ways, **Harold** had one more thing to say to Paul. And it sounded ominous.

"It won't be long before there won't be any choice about joining. Remember that."

CHAPTER 2

Thursday, September 1, 1938

The next day, Paul walked to school alone. Harold had left earlier to meet up with some of the other boys from his Hitler Youth group. Their conversation from the previous day still snaked its way through Paul's brain. He had not stopped thinking about it since the moment he had arrived home. Even his parents seemed to sense that something was preoccupying him.

"There must be something troubling you," his mother commented as Paul absentmindedly moved food around his dinner plate, his head propped up with one hand. "You're not eating."

"Yes, what is it?" his father asked. Paul had the same piercing blue eyes as his father and the same deep dimple in his cheek that seemed to get deeper whenever he was upset. In this moment, it looked like a crater had formed on Papa's face.

Paul never liked to worry his parents. They were both doctors, working long hours at St. Martin's hospital in the city center. Mama was an obstetrician, often delivering babies late into the night. She said it was the perfect medical specialty for her. "I get to bring new life into the world almost every day."

Papa was an orthopedist, specializing in bone and joint disorders. He had set Paul's leg into a cast the time he flung himself across the finish line of the year-end school race. He had won the race but couldn't run again for months after the break.

Paul shook his head and straightened, forcing a bite of the beef stew that Mama had made. He smiled briefly at his parents. "Just a lot of schoolwork to think about."

Mama frowned. She had a line of freckles across her nose that Paul had inherited. Mama often understood what people were thinking and feeling without having to ask. She often read Paul's mind, pushing him to talk even when he was in a bad mood. But today Paul didn't want to talk. He figured he could sort out his problem with Harold and the Nazi Youth on his own. Luckily, Mama was preoccupied with a difficult birth that she'd supervised at the hospital. A moment later, she went back to talking about her day and left Paul alone.

The school bell was already ringing as Paul sprinted

the last block to school and joined the line that marched silently into the building. Even though it was early morning, the classroom was already stifling hot. The school year started in mid-August for all German children. This meant that it would be uncomfortable inside all day long. The building seemed to suck in the air from outside and hold it like a giant hot-air balloon. It would be another month before things began to cool down.

Everyone was quiet as their teacher, Herr Bentz, called the class to order. Today, there was another lesson on what he referred to as racial science, more specifically: how to distinguish a superior German from an inferior Jew. To begin the lecture, Herr Bentz read from a book called *The Poisonous Mushroom*. "It's a picture book. Some of you may think it's too young. But it's a wonderful story," he said, "that teaches us all a valuable lesson."

The book, he explained, was about a mother and her young son who were gathering mushrooms in the German forest. The boy found some poisonous ones and his mother warned him that there are good mushrooms and deadly ones. As they walked home, she said:

"Look, my son, human beings in this world are like the mushrooms in the forest. There are good mushrooms and there are good people. There are poisonous, bad mushrooms and there are bad people. And do you know who these bad people are—these poisonous mushrooms of humankind?"

Her son slapped his chest in pride. "Of course, I know, Mother! They are the Jews!"

The students in Paul's class laughed out loud when Herr Bentz read that part. Their teacher beamed. "Yes, I see you all understand that comparison." Then, he called Harold to the front of the classroom and instructed him to draw the number six on the blackboard. "And make it big," he added.

Harold picked up the chalk and drew a large number six in the middle of the board. Then, Herr Bentz told him to sit down. The teacher picked up the wooden pointer and ran it over the number that Harold had drawn. "Do you see this shape?" he asked. "Do you see how round and hooked it is?"

The students shouted, "Yes, Herr Bentz!"

"Well, the Jewish nose is crooked at its tip, just like the Jew himself is crooked. His nose looks just like this number six."

The students roared with laughter once more. And the more the others in his class laughed, the more upset and agitated Paul became. He looked around. There were no longer any Jewish students in Paul's class. Their number had been dwindling ever since Hitler had introduced his "Law Against the Overcrowding of German Schools." But now, they were completely gone, as well as all the Jewish teachers. Paul didn't know where or if any of them were now in other schools. All he knew was that he had arrived in school one day and there were no Jewish students to be seen. He wondered about them now as Herr Bentz carried on with the lesson. He thought about one person in particular, a Jewish girl named Analia Morgenstern.

Paul and Analia had been friends since childhood. Analia lived in the Kasernenstrasse district of Düsseldorf, an area where many Jewish people lived, and many Jewish businesses were located. Her mother was also a doctor and a close friend of Paul's parents. In fact, it was Paul's parents who had convinced Analia's mother to send her to Paul's school, believing it was the best school in Düsseldorf, even though it was further from Analia's home. Paul and Analia had often sat for lunch together in the schoolyard and had done homework together when their parents were working late. Paul could talk with Analia more easily than with anyone else, easier than he could talk to Harold. She understood him, laughed at his bad jokes, and reasoned with him if he was in a foul mood. There was even that kiss that they had shared a couple of summers ago by Lake Kaarst.

It had been a beautiful Saturday afternoon when they had hopped on their bicycles for the forty-five-minute ride to the lake, taking the Oberkassel Bridge to cross the Rhine River, and continuing west of Düsseldorf. The beach was a scenic spot about fifteen kilometers from the city. Paul had been going there with his family for years, a perfect location to escape the oppressive summer heat. The coarse, sandy beach, about the size of a soccer field, was bordered on either side by dense forest. Wheat-colored reeds grew by the water's edge. On blustery days, the reeds waved and brushed against one another, sounding as if they were whispering. Today, on this windless day, they were still. Paul and Analia were hot and sweaty by the time they arrived. Sunlight poured down from a cloudless sky, and gray and white geese squawked at the side of the water, while bathers splashed and dove under the gentle lapping waves. A group of men kicked a soccer ball back and forth on the sand.

Paul and Analia chose a spot far from everyone else. They spread a blanket onto the sand and stripped down to their bathing suits. Analia ran to the water first, but Paul had no difficulty catching up and passing her. He dove in cleanly, cleaving the water with hardly a splash. Then, with long strokes, he pulled himself along the sandy bottom until his lungs cried out for air and he surfaced, flinging the drops of water off his head. He looked around. Analia was floating on her back some distance away, face up to the sun, eyes closed. Paul couldn't resist. He dove underneath her, and positioned himself directly below her stretched-out body. Then he raised his arms, pushed his feet against the sandy bottom, and thrust Analia high up into the air. She flailed, yelped out loud, and landed with a tremendous splash, arms and legs flapping in all directions. She came up gasping for air. Paul wasn't sure if she would be angry with him, but she wasn't. She sputtered a few times, looked at Paul, and then burst out laughing, scooping handfuls of water and throwing them back into his face. They were both cold and shaking by the time they emerged from the lake an hour later.

Back on the beach, they shared the cheese sandwiches that Analia's mother had packed for them and then lay back on the blanket, letting the sun warm their bodies. It was a perfect day. Analia was the first one to talk about the dangers that Jews in Düsseldorf were beginning to face.

"Things are getting worse for us; for Jews, I mean," Analia said, still lying on her back, eyes remaining closed. "My mother is only allowed to treat Jewish people right now. And she thinks it won't be long before she isn't allowed to practice medicine at all."

Paul raised himself up on one elbow to look over at her. "What will she do if that happens?"

Analia shrugged. "It's not as if she has any say in it. And it's not like she can get another job if she loses this one. There aren't many people who will hire a Jewish person for any job. And my father is just as worried about his position in his law firm. It's happening to Jews everywhere."

Paul didn't know how to respond. Saying "I'm sorry" just wasn't enough.

"The crazy thing is, we've always considered ourselves to be loyal German citizens—proud of our country. And now, the country is telling us we're not good enough. It doesn't make sense." Analia brought her hands up to cover her face. "I don't want to talk about this anymore. I don't know why I brought it up in the first place." She sighed. "I just want to enjoy this day."

That was when she suddenly sat up and faced Paul. "I know you want to kiss me," she said.

That statement came out of the blue! Paul stared at her—her rounded cheeks tinged with red from the sun, her intense hazel eyes and long brown hair, still damp from the lake water. His face grew red.

"Do not!" he protested.

"Do so. You've wanted to kiss me since forever. Admit it."

It was true, but he wasn't about to tell her that. He could feel the heat from his cheeks creeping up his face and into his hairline. His whole head was hot, and it wasn't from the sun.

Analia suddenly looked shy and dropped her eyes. She chewed absently on a nail. "The thing is," she said, "I'd like to kiss you, too."

Shyness gone, she made the first move, leaning toward Paul and pressing her lips against his. The kiss lasted no more than a second. But in that instant, the fire in Paul's face swept through his body.

★ ★ ★

Herr Bentz's loud voice brought Paul back into the classroom.

"What else do we know about Jews?" Herr Bentz was asking.

"Jews don't care about Germany," one girl declared. "They only care if things go well for themselves. They have no business being among us true Germans."

Herr Bentz nodded. "Very good. What else?"

"And they cheat," another student said. "Everyone knows that."

"Correct," Herr Bentz declared. "But Jews are not the only enemy of the state. Who else should we be wary of?"

The hands in the classroom shot up. Herr Bentz selected Ernst Wagner, a boy with whom Paul wasn't particularly friendly but who lived directly across the street from him. "We shouldn't trust anyone who speaks out against our glorious Führer," Ernst stated.

"And what would you do if it was one of your parents who spoke against the government? What if they said that the Führer will be defeated one day—or that we shouldn't listen to him?" Herr Bentz looked around the room at hands that waved in the air. "Ernst?"

"We can't allow that kind of talk in Germany," Ernst said.

"Of course not. It's dangerous. Subversive. So, what would you do if your parents spoke those words?"

Ernst stood up from his desk and puffed out his chest, pulling his shoulders back. "I would not hesitate to turn them in."

"Well said! Germany and the Führer must always come first, above friends and even family," Herr Bentz declared as the students in the class applauded enthusiastically.

Paul squirmed in his seat and looked around again. Was he the only one who was troubled by the spell that Hitler had cast across the country? A few other students seemed uncomfortable as well. They had their heads down or turned away from the conversation. But most of the students had joined in, enthusiastically. Paul couldn't wait until the bell rang and he could get out of class. But, before leaving at the end of the day, Herr Bentz stopped him and motioned for him to come to his desk. Paul stood nervously in front of his teacher. He hadn't answered any questions all day. He hadn't raised his hand or cheered along with the other students. Was he going to be questioned?

Herr Bentz let Paul squirm for a moment before finally speaking. "You are a strong young man, a gifted athlete, and a real asset to this school and our country."

"Thank you, Herr Bentz," Paul said cautiously.

"I understand you have not yet signed up for the Hitler Youth," Herr Bentz said.

Who had told him that? Harold? Ernst? Someone from the Hitler Youth who kept track of these things and reported them? "No, Herr Bentz," he stuttered. "I'm still…I'm still thinking about it."

A large picture of Adolf Hitler hung above Herr Bentz's desk. The Führer's eyes bore down on Paul as if he were there in the room, watching him, waiting for an answer, or at the very least, expecting a salute. Paul looked away.

Herr Bentz leaned back, pursed his lips, and brought his hands up to his mouth, still scrutinizing Paul with narrowed eyes. Finally, he took a deep breath and sat up in his chair. "Well, while you're thinking I'd like you to write an essay for me entitled 'Why Am I Not in the Hitler Youth.' Perhaps that will help with your decision-making. You can hand it in to me later this week."

CHAPTER 3

The warm outside air floating across his face was a welcome relief for Paul as he fled the stifling classroom and left the school building. Even though he had avoided any punishment from Herr Bentz for failing to participate in the class discussion, the thought of having to write an essay on why he hadn't joined the Hitler Youth hung over him. What was he going to say? How could he tread that fine line of appearing to be loyal to Hitler on the one hand, and explaining his reluctance to join up?

He spotted Harold walking with Ernst ahead and sped up to catch them. He still couldn't believe that Ernst had said that he would turn in his own parents if he caught them speaking out against the government.

Ernst was in an animated conversation with Harold, still talking about the difference between Jews and "good" Germans. Ernst had the kind of booming voice that could be heard across any schoolyard. And he had a frame to match his tone: he was tall with solid, muscular arms. His shoulders were so broad that it always looked as if his shirt would pop its buttons if he breathed too deeply.

"That was an inspiring lecture from Herr Bentz today, didn't you think so, Ritter?" Ernst called everyone by their last name.

Paul glared at him; he couldn't help himself, and Ernst was quick to catch his look.

"What's eating you?"

"Would you really turn in your parents?" Paul blurted.

"Of course! Anyone who makes a statement that harms the welfare or reputation of the government is to be punished."

Ernst was quoting a decree that had been issued by the Nazis several years earlier. "But we're talking about your parents, Ernst," Paul protested. "Not some guy on the street who might be ranting against the government."

Ernst snorted. "What's the difference? The law is the law. No one is above it."

Paul turned his face away before he said something that might get him into trouble. Who knew what Ernst was capable of doing?

"Herr Bentz made some other excellent points in class today, don't you think?" Ernst was still talking, but Paul was in no mood to answer. Ernst turned instead to Harold.

"Becker?" Ernst asked. "What did you think of what Herr Bentz said today?"

Harold had been quiet on the walk home and now answered weakly, "Not all Jews have noses like Herr Bentz said they did."

Ernst laughed. "Most of them do!"

How ignorant, Paul thought, but he was impressed that Harold had tried, albeit softly, to stand up to Ernst. "Doesn't it bother you that all the Jews have left our school?" Paul asked. "It's as though they disappeared into thin air."

Ernst shook his head. "Why should it bother me? Besides, they haven't just disappeared. A lot of them have been taken away."

Ernst was referring to the concentration camps. Herr Bentz had talked several times about those prisons; places like Oranienburg, north of Berlin, and Dachau, northwest of Munich, and other locations where Jews had been sent and were being starved, tortured, and used as forced labor.

Paul had no idea what had happened to Analia and her family. After that day in the summer, she had stopped wanting to go to the beach with him. In fact, she stopped trying to see him at all. At first, Paul thought she might be angry or upset with him after their kiss. But, as the list of laws and rules restricting Jews grew, Paul finally faced the truth that her disappearance from his life was about more than just the two of them. When the next school year began and Analia and the other Jewish students were absent, Paul had tried to find her. His mother confirmed that Analia's mother was no longer working at the hospital.

Once, Paul had ridden his bicycle past Analia's apartment just to see if she was there. He knew she lived on the first floor of a small building. The curtains of her flat were drawn and it looked as if the building might be deserted. Paul stood outside, across the street, staring at the draped windows. A few minutes later, someone pulled the curtain back slightly to look outside. Paul's heart lifted. Hoping it was Analia, he raised his arm to wave. But whoever it was at the window shut the curtains tightly, as if they didn't want to be seen. He finally dropped his arm, climbed back on his bicycle, and rode away.

Had Analia and her family been taken away to one of those concentration camps? Paul prayed not.

"Anyway, they're just Jews, so who cares what happens to them?" Ernst's booming voice cut through Paul's thoughts.

Paul couldn't stand another minute of this conversation. Luckily, they were approaching their respective homes. All he wanted to do was lie on his bed, close his eyes, and forget about Herr Bentz, Ernst, and the Hitler Youth.

He said a quick good-bye to Harold and Ernst and bounded up the lane to his house. At the door, he stopped short. There was still that essay he had to write for his teacher.

CHAPTER 4

Saturday, September 3, 1938

A couple of days later, Harold finally convinced Paul to join him at a Hitler Youth meeting. Paul had already realized that he didn't have much choice. Not to go might arouse too much attention. Herr Bentz had questioned him, and now Ernst was looking at him strangely. It didn't help that each morning began with Herr Bentz asking his students what they had seen or heard. There was often at least one informant who was willing to speak up.

"This shop keeper didn't give the Hitler salute when a parade passed by his shop."

"This woman stopped to help an old Jewish man when the police were interrogating him."

"I heard a woman in the market say that she hoped Hitler would stop passing more laws."

The list of violations that the students reported grew in number each day, and Herr Bentz's praise for his students' actions grew along with it. It was as if Paul's classmates had become spies for the Nazi government. It left Paul feeling numb and scared. He and Harold talked about it again as they walked home from school.

"Just come with me to a meeting," Harold pleaded. He was relentless in his efforts to get Paul to join him.

Paul shook his head. "I told you, it's not for me."

"You don't have to sign up, at least not yet. But just show them that you're being respectful. That's enough for now."

That was when Paul decided he would go. Harold was right. It was better to be seen going along with the others than to keep resisting. Paul was increasingly afraid that he'd become the subject of another one of those morning reports in school.

There's a boy in our class who refuses to be part of the Hitler Youth.

Paul imagined Ernst standing up, pointing at him, and declaring this transgression. Harold was a true friend and would never turn on him, Paul thought. But Ernst was another story.

The only thing good about deciding to go to the meeting was that it got him off the hook with Herr

Bentz's essay. When he told his teacher about his plans, Herr Bentz smiled broadly and slapped him on the back.

"That's the spirit! Go to a meeting! See how inspiring they are. We'll put aside the essay, for now."

Herr Bentz didn't question him further about actually signing up. Perhaps this would be enough to get his teacher off his back—at least for the time being.

The Hitler Youth meetings were held every Saturday morning in a fairground on the other side of the Rhine River, across the Oberkassel Bridge, sometimes on other days as well. And they started early, at 7:00 a.m.

"It's good training to be up at the crack of dawn," Harold had said.

Getting up early on a Saturday morning was one more reason for Paul to dread this! But he had promised Harold he would go, so he joined him, and the two boys biked to the fairground. Dozens of boys were already gathered when Paul and Harold arrived. The field was aflame with masses of flags fluttering in the breeze: black swastikas on blood-red backgrounds. Paul shuddered. Someone was standing on a platform at one end of the field, a megaphone in his hand, ordering everyone to assemble in rows. Silently and efficiently, the boys took their places as Paul looked around. Most of the others were wearing the uniform of the Hitler Youth: brown short-sleeved shirt, black tie, brown knee-length shorts, and brown boots that came up to the ankle. Paul shifted uncomfortably and clasped his sweaty hands behind his back. He felt painfully out of place, not only because of his civilian clothes and long hair, but because his body was crying out to leave. He was regretting the decision to come, even before the meeting got underway.

"Sieg Heil!" the young man at the megaphone shouted.

Arms thrust up into the air in a salute to Adolf Hitler as everyone around Paul shouted "hail to victory" in reply. Paul had no choice but to raise his arm as well. It felt like a betrayal of all that he believed in.

"We are preparing all of you to become young soldiers in our military," the man at the megaphone continued.

There it was again, the idea that this was a call to arms. No messages about the importance of justice for all, no inspiring ideas about the value of going to school or doing good deeds for others. The boys around Paul raised their arms in salute.

Paul looked over at Harold whose eyes were lit up with joy. He glanced down the row of boys and spotted Ernst, his face animated and shining, his voice thundering above the others. Paul dropped his arm limply by his side.

The young man with the megaphone began to move down the rows of boys, stopping here and there to inspect a uniform or praise someone who stood at attention. Now and then, he ordered a boy to step forward as he bellowed a warning about some infraction.

"Your boots are dirty. Make sure they are clean the next time you come."

"Your shirt is creased. You look like you just rolled out of bed. Iron it for next time."

"Straighten up. No slouching at these meetings."

Each boy who was admonished shouted, "Yes, *Fähnleinführer*." They referred to the young officer as "troop leader." Then, they raised their arms again and stepped back into line.

The officer paused in front of Harold, studying him intently. "Well done!" he finally said. "You're a credit to the movement."

Harold beamed like he'd been handed the best gift of his life. "Thank you, troop leader!"

Paul's stomach was in nervous knots as the young officer moved over to him. His eyes traveled from Paul's long hair to his rumpled shorts and scuffed shoes, a hardened expression on his face, eyes half-closed.

"You're new," he said. He was not much older than Paul but carried himself with the authority of someone who liked to be in charge. "Your name?"

At first, Paul's mouth felt too dry to be able to speak.

"Paul Ritter," he finally croaked. His tongue stuck to the roof of his mouth.

The troop leader nodded. "I see you are not in uniform. Why have you not joined up?"

There was that never-ending question again. Paul hated it. The nerves he had felt seconds earlier turned to irritation. An angry weight grew in his chest.

"Is there a law that says I have to be a member?"

Paul regretted the words as soon as they were out of his mouth. Harold gasped. The young officer's eyes narrowed again. His face stiffened and a muscle twitched beside his right eye. Paul closed his eyes, half expecting the officer to scream at him or order him to leave, or something worse that he couldn't even imagine.

But when he opened his eyes a moment later, the troop leader was grinning. "I like a young lad with nerve," he said as Paul tried to breathe again. "And you're right; it's not mandatory to join us." Then, he leaned forward until his mouth was close to Paul's ear, and he whispered, "At least, not yet!"

Paul was quiet during the bike ride home. His head was full of images of his peers singing songs to Adolf Hitler, shouting his name and saluting, worked up into a frenzy. He had never seen anything like it in his life! He pumped his feet on the bike pedals, feeling the sweat begin to roll down his back. The anxiety and stiffness he had felt at the meeting began to seep away with each thrust of the pedals. Harold was behind him. Paul could almost hear him puffing and struggling to keep up. Finally, Paul slowed and got off his bike, motioning Harold to do the same. The two boys walked side by side.

"I don't think you should have talked back to Franz," Harold said breaking the silence, still breathing heavily from the bike ride. That was the name of the young officer, Franz Fischer. "You could have made him really mad."

Paul sighed. "Tell me again why you want to be part of a group like that."

Harold shrugged and reached up to wipe his forehead. He was sweating hard from the bike ride. "They make me feel I'm important."

Paul understood that. It was not that Harold was someone who was routinely picked on. In many ways, his friendship with Paul had protected him from being harassed. But he was known as one of the less popular kids in the class, and often excluded from activities, or the last one chosen to be part of any team. Now, he had a ready-made group of friends who waited for him at school, walked with him to meetings, and included him in conversations. And he had young officers like Franz Fischer telling him that he was the future of the country.

"Even Ernst has been nice to me," Harold continued. "And he never used to talk to me before all of this."

Ernst had disappeared from the Hitler Youth meeting as soon as Franz had dismissed everyone. That suited Paul just fine. The last thing he wanted was to have Ernst biking home alongside him and Harold, bellowing out praises for the meeting and everyone who had been there. It was hard enough having to listen to Harold.

"Ernst is a bully," Paul insisted. "He's just using you."

Harold shook his head. "That's not true. He's really not a bad guy. He's become my friend."

Paul stopped pushing his bike and whirled to face Harold. "You're fooling yourself! Why can't you see that? Ernst may be nice to you today, and the Nazis might make you feel important right now, but they'll turn on you in a second."

"I don't believe that," Harold protested.

And they put everyone else down. Paul didn't say those words aloud. He was thinking about Analia again. He wondered where she was and worried about whether she was safe.

"Look at what Hitler has done for our country," Harold insisted. "Our schools are better. People are at work earning good money. There's food on every table and clothes in every closet. Those are all good things."

Paul sighed again. "That's just what everyone said

when Hitler came to power. *'Oh, he's so great! He's brought us jobs. Kids have food to eat.'"*

Harold nodded. "That's right! That's exactly what he's done."

"And meanwhile, if you say anything bad about him or if you don't want to salute his flag, you'll be thrown in jail."

"I don't think that's really happening," Harold protested.

"Of course it is! You know that new boy in our class? The one who came from Cologne. He told me his father was put in jail for a week because he refused to fly a Nazi flag in front of his store. How is that good? And how is it okay for Hitler to treat Jewish people and others like garbage?"

Harold was quiet. Paul knew he wasn't going to win this argument, and continuing the fight only made Paul's head hurt. He was disturbed enough by the meeting they'd left. This exchange with his friend only added to his distress.

The two boys continued to push their bikes in silence, until they finally rounded a corner close to their homes. There was only one more block to go. Paul couldn't wait to get home. He felt a need to talk to his parents about all of this. He had avoided saying much to them up until now. But it was time to sit down with them and try and make sense of it all.

"What's going on up ahead?" Harold voice cut through Paul's thoughts.

There was some kind of commotion close to Paul's house. People from the neighborhood had gathered outside, lining both sides of the street. A long black car flying the swastika flag from its hood was parked on the road. Next to it was an open-back truck with two soldiers standing guard, holding rifles. Paul's heart began to pound. For a moment, he thought this had something to do with his parents. Were they in trouble? Was this because of what he had said to Franz at the meeting? No, that was impossible. The meeting had just ended. Paul picked up his pace, eyes aimed ahead. His bike pedal whacked against his ankle and a searing pain rose up his leg. He winced and pushed forward. It was only when he had pulled up to his house that he realized that the vehicles were not in front of his home. They were parked next to Ernst's place.

As Paul and Harold watched, the door to Ernst's house opened. A moment later, his parents, Frau and Herr Wagner, walked out holding each other. Their heads were lowered. Ernst's mother was crying. A Nazi officer followed them out the door and escorted them to the truck. They climbed up onto the flatbed under the watchful eyes of the two soldiers with rifles.

Paul glanced back at Ernst's front door and that's when he saw Ernst. He was standing there in the doorway with his grandmother next to him. Her face was ashen and lined with tears. But when Paul glanced at Ernst, his heart went cold. Ernst's face was flat, hard, and emotionless.

Paul's stomach sank with the realization of what was happening. Ernst had reported his parents to the authorities for something—who knew what! Whatever it was, his parents were being taken away. This was just what Ernst had bragged about doing, what Herr Bentz had applauded him for declaring.

Paul could hear Harold fighting for breath next to him. When Paul turned to him, Harold's face was pasty and he looked as if he might pass out.

"Do you still think Ernst is a good friend?" Paul asked.

Harold's eyes widened.

The truck suddenly revved its engine and drove off down the block, turning a corner on two squealing tires. The black car followed close behind. That's when Paul turned to look at Ernst still standing in the doorway of his house. Ernst shifted and caught Paul's eye, returning his look with a cold, dark stare. Then, Ernst turned and walked back inside, closing the door behind him.

Without saying another word to Harold, Paul dropped his bicycle on the ground and bolted up the walkway to his own house. He pushed open the door and ran inside calling out for his parents. They were in the sitting room at the front of the house looking out the front window, clutching one another as if each needed the support of the other. They had witnessed the whole thing.

"I'm so relieved you're home!" Paul's mother cried.

"Ernst turned his parents in," Paul said, still stunned. "His own parents!"

Mama shook her head. "It's unthinkable. They're good people, kind and thoughtful."

"This is beyond what we ever imagined. What is happening in our country?" Paul's father asked this as if he were speaking to himself.

"I can't imagine what made Ernst do this," Mama continued.

"I know why he did it," Paul said angrily. "It's what our teachers are telling us to do. It's what the government expects us to do."

"But his own parents…." Mama's voice trailed off into a whisper.

"What's going to happen to them?" Paul asked.

"They'll be interrogated," Papa said. "It's the Gestapo that's in charge of those things, the secret police of the Nazi government. They're meant to stop what they call 'criminal activity against the state.' Their powers are limitless. I've heard that they can be harsh. They try to extract information any way they can." His eyes blazed. "After the questioning, who knows what will happen...?" The unfinished statement dangled in the air.

Paul and his parents stood in the room, staring out the window. There was no one on the street now. Everyone had disappeared behind closed doors. It now looked as calm and peaceful as if nothing had happened. The only evidence of anything unusual was Paul's bicycle, abandoned on the side of the road, one wheel still spinning in circles.

"Do you think they'll come back?" Paul finally asked. "Ernst's parents, I mean."

No one answered.

CHAPTER 5
Saturday, September 10, 1938

Paul stayed up late into the night, talking with his parents about everything that had happened. It felt like the first open and honest conversation they had had in months. They talked about Hitler and how he was persuading the nation to follow his fanatical ideas. They talked about his hatred for Jews and how he had always blamed them for any problems that Germany had. They talked about attacks against Jews, not only in Düsseldorf but in other cities as well.

"There's a synagogue in Munich that was destroyed by Nazi thugs just a couple of months ago," Papa said, shaking his head.

And they talked about how loyalty to Hitler had becomes more important than anything else in current-day Germany.

"Ernst turned his own parents over to the authorities," Paul whispered for the umpteenth time. He couldn't shake the image of Frau Wagner and her husband being led from their house, clutching one another as if their lives depended on it. He couldn't forget the look on Ernst's face, blank and emotionless, while he watched his parents being taken away.

"No one is safe," Mama said.

"No one," Papa echoed.

It was the incident with the Wagners that convinced Paul's parents that he must join the Hitler Youth. They were afraid for him. He fought his parents on this with all his might.

"We've just finished talking about how evil Hitler is and how the kids in the Youth group are just his puppets. And now you want me to become one of them?" He had been thinking about ways to oppose the Hitler Youth—some way he could speak out against what was happening, especially to young people in his country. And now, his parents were telling him to sign up. What were they thinking?

"It's not that we want this for you," his father argued back. "But it may be the best way to keep you safe. These days, we all have to find ways to avoid trouble.

Even your Mama and I need to be careful of what we say when we're in public. You have to at least try and go along with them."

"Even if you're just pretending," Mama added.

"Yes," Papa said. "Just be respectful."

It was exactly what Harold had been telling him, although in the last day or so Harold had become more jittery and less self-assured than before. It was as if the arrest of Ernst's parents had also sparked something in Harold that made him realize how dangerous the whole organization could be.

In the end, Paul stopped arguing with his parents and agreed that he would officially join. His mother cut his hair the evening before the meeting where he would be sworn in. Neither said much as she lovingly brushed the mop of curls off his forehead and then cropped them away with scissors. Blond tresses floated to the floor like dandelion fluff in a spring breeze. *It's only hair*, Paul repeated in his mind. *It doesn't mean anything.* And yet, when he saw himself in the mirror after Mama had finished, the face reflected back looked so much like that of one of the Hitler Youth that Paul nearly choked.

And when he stood once more in front of the mirror, dressed in the uniform that his parents had just bought for him, he barely recognized himself. His parents were waiting at the front door to say good-bye.

Mama slipped the arm band with the swastika symbol on his arm and adjusted it. Her eyes were downcast, and her lips trembled. "Don't forget who you really are," she whispered as she hugged him tightly.

Papa shook Paul's hand. His face was drawn and tense. "It's what's in your heart that matters. Not the clothes you wear."

Those were the words ringing in Paul's ears as he headed out the door. Harold was waiting for him. They rode their bicycles part way to the fairground for the meeting but decided to get off and push their bikes for the last part of the trip. On the way, they passed a billboard that read: *Are you a German boy? Come join our group of young people.* And then another less inviting one that read: *Jews are not wanted here or anywhere.*

Harold was quiet as they walked side by side.

"Are you okay?" Paul finally asked.

Harold turned his head to look at him. "I'm not sure. I thought I knew what I was doing. And I still think it's the right thing for you to join up—for both of us to be part of it. But nothing makes much sense anymore."

"That's exactly what I've been trying to tell you. It doesn't make sense!"

"But what are we supposed to do?" Harold asked, eyes pleading as they turned to Paul. "We have to be part of the Hitler Youth. We have to obey the rules. You saw them take away Ernst's parents. I don't want that to happen to my family—or yours!"

Paul shook his head. "I don't know what the answer is. But there's got to be a way to resist all of this."

"I don't think there is," Harold replied. "They're too powerful for us."

"Sometimes I wonder if we all banded together, we could stand up as a group and fight against the Ernsts of Germany," said Paul. "Maybe that would make a difference."

Harold's eyes widened.

"Don't worry," Paul said. "I said I'd join up and I'm here, aren't I?"

The boys had arrived at the fairground. They deposited their bikes to one side and moved into the crowd.

The new boys were being called to assemble on the platform at one end of the field. Paul left Harold and climbed the stairs to join five other boys, each one with closely cropped hair like his, each wearing a new, crisply ironed uniform. The same troop leader, Franz Fischer, had his megaphone in hand and quieted the crowd.

"These young men," he began, waving his arm over the heads of Paul and the other five, "your friends, are joining us today in our glorious mission to serve Germany and our great Führer."

The boys in the crowd roared their approval. Out of the corner of his eye, Paul caught Ernst standing in the crowd, whistling and whooping louder than anyone else. Paul quickly looked away, trying his hardest to breathe evenly.

Franz turned to face the new recruits. "You are our nation's most precious future. Never forget that one day you will rule the world!"

The cheers were even more deafening.

"And now, each young man will begin by taking the official oath of the Hitler Youth."

With that, Franz moved to stand in front of the first boy in the row, handing him a swastika flag and ordering that he raise his arm in a salute to Hitler. The oath done, he moved to the second boy, then the third and so on. When it was Paul's turn, Franz thrust the flag in his direction. Paul grasped it with his left hand, and shakily raised his right arm to the sky.

"In the presence of this blood banner which represents our Führer," he repeated after Franz, "I swear to devote all my energies and my strength to the savior of our country, Adolf Hitler. I am willing and ready to give up my life for him." Paul nearly gagged on the words as he fought, with all his might, the urge to turn and run.

Franz looked approvingly at him. "Glad you decided to join us," he said. "It was the smart thing to do."

CHAPTER 6

Saturday, September 10, 1938

The rest of that meeting passed like a bad dream for Paul.
There were more oaths, more songs of praise to Hitler,
and more shouts of "Sieg Heil!" Paul moved through it
all like a machine on automatic pilot. When the meeting
finally ended, he jumped back on his bicycle with Harold
at his side and rode home at a pace to rival a speeding car.
He leaned forward on the pedals and pumped as hard
as he could, feeling the sweat roll down his back and
dampen the new uniform. He knew that Harold must be
struggling to keep up with him. When he finally glanced
over his shoulder, his friend was nowhere to be seen.
But in that moment, Paul didn't care. He needed to ride
like mad so that he could rid his body of all the furious
energy he had been holding in during the meeting.

Mama sat him down when he got home and made him tell her everything he could remember. "The more you talk, the better you'll feel after," she said. Paul wasn't sure he really felt better at the end of their conversation. But, by the time he went to bed, he was exhausted. He slept soundly through the night and woke up feeling better.

But that feeling didn't last long. There was another meeting scheduled for the next afternoon and the bike ride to the fairground with Harold filled Paul with the same dread he'd experienced the day before. Up ahead, they could see a bonfire raging in a pit close to the stage where Paul had been sworn in. Several boys were gathered around the fire, adding more wood to feed it, then poking at the logs with long sticks.

"What now?" Paul asked under his breath.

"I don't like the looks of this," Harold added.

It didn't take long to find out what the plan was for the meeting. Franz called everyone to order, wielding his megaphone as he always did. The meeting started with praise to Adolf Hitler and the usual salute. Then, Franz faced the boys.

"Today, you will all undergo a test of courage," he began. Then he explained that one by one, the boys would be expected to run toward the firepit and jump over it. "Germany must have fearless young people to protect it and keep it strong. This test will determine if you are one of those daring people."

Paul looked over at the firepit. The flames surged into the air easily reaching to his shoulders. It would take a strong runner and an even stronger jumper to clear the blaze.

"I don't think I can do this," Harold whispered. When Paul glanced over at him, his eyes were bulging, and his face had gone white.

"You can!" Paul urged. "Just watch the others and see how they're doing it. Watch me. If you have to, jump to the side so you're not really going over the top of the fire. No one will notice."

Harold swallowed hard and nodded.

"Line up!" Franz instructed as the boys eagerly fell into a line. The first boy to go was Ernst, practically dancing on his toes to show his readiness to jump. On Franz's command, Ernst ran toward the fire, leapt high into the air, and cleared the pit easily. He pumped his fist in the air as everyone cheered. Franz nodded his approval.

The second boy in line jumped easily as well, as did the third, and the fourth. The fifth boy was smaller and scrawny looking; legs as thin as reeds and a uniform that looked a couple of sizes too big. His name was Max. He stared at the fire a long time before finally taking a deep breath and running toward it, waving his wiry arms to gather speed. As he approached the pit, he veered suddenly to one side, clearing the lowest part of the fire, but not able to get over the top of it. It was exactly what Paul had told Harold to do. But Paul also said that no one would notice, and on that point he was wrong.

"You," Franz bellowed, pointing a finger at the small boy. "Go back and do it again. And this time, do it right. I won't have cheaters in this group."

Paul heard Harold suck in his breath behind him. He turned toward him. "I know you can do this! Just focus and run as fast as you can. Don't think twice."

Max returned to the line to try the jump again. He ran toward the pit, gathering speed. But at the last second, he hesitated. As he jumped into the air, the fire grazed his back leg and he landed on the other side of the pit yelping and holding his leg. The boys began to laugh. Franz quieted them with a glare.

"He's a brave soldier," Franz yelled into his megaphone. "He did it again and did it to the best of his ability. No fear. I want that kind of young man in my unit." Max beamed and limped back into line.

Now it was Paul's turn. He took a deep breath and began to run toward the fire. He thrust his right leg up and out, as if he were running a race and about to clear a hurdle. Then he propelled his body and cleared the fire with no difficulty. When he glanced at Franz, the troop leader nodded his approval.

Harold was next in line. Paul caught his eye, giving him an encouraging nod and firm thumbs-up. Harold looked terrified.

"Next," Franz shouted.

Harold didn't budge.

"I said move! Now!"

Still nothing.

A third order came from Franz and, finally, Harold began to run toward the fire. Paul could tell he was in trouble before his feet left the ground.

The jump was too low. As Harold tried desperately to clear the fire, it seemed to reach up and grab him, wrapping its flames tightly around his leg. He screamed and collapsed on the ground on the other side, rolling first one way and then the other, holding on to his injured leg. The smell of charred flesh filled the air. When Harold moved his hands away, Paul could see that the burned skin had pulled away and left a wound that was raw and gaping. Harold's eyes were wild and frantic with pain.

No one moved. Everyone stared at Harold on the ground, writhing and moaning. Finally, Franz approached and stood over him.

"Let me see!" Franz commanded.

Tears streamed down Harold's face as he allowed Franz to take a look.

"You'll be fine," Franz declared. "And there's no place

for tears in the Hitler Youth!" With that, he turned and marched away, giving the order to the next boy in line to jump the pit.

Paul was just about to rush over to help his friend when someone grabbed his arm. He whirled around to face Ernst, a giant smirk on his face. He leaned forward to Paul. "He's weak," Ernst said, pointing at Harold, still on the ground. "Not like you and me. He'll never become a soldier."

CHAPTER 7
Saturday, September 17, 1938

It took more than a week for Harold's leg to heal. In the meantime, he was given permission to miss several of the Hitler Youth meetings. Without the company of his good friend, Paul found the meetings more unbearable than ever. He hated the songs they sang to glorify Hitler. He hated having to salute the flag with his arm outstretched. Even the physical training—the sit-ups, chin lifts, and push-ups that at any other time he would have found challenging and even enjoyable—he hated. And he hated the suggestions to turn on his neighbors if they didn't support the Nazi party. Participating in these meetings gave Paul the sense that he was betraying everything he believed. He tried to remember his father's words: *It's what's in your heart that matters.* That was what kept him going.

He stayed away from Ernst as much as he could, though that wasn't always possible. With Harold absent, Ernst seemed to think that Paul was his new best friend. He waited for him to cycle to meetings, stood next to him during the oath taking, and tried to cycle home together afterward. Whenever Ernst tried to engage him in conversation—usually about how great a leader Hitler was—Paul managed to change the topic or avoid answering with a shrug of his shoulders.

One afternoon, Paul noticed Ernst's parents returning home. They had been gone for days. Paul had wondered what had happened to them after their arrest. Ernst had never said a word about it. Paul watched as what appeared to be the same black automobile with the swastika flag flying from its hood pulled up to Ernst's house. The back door opened, and Frau and Herr Wagner climbed out and walked slowly up the path to their front door. Their heads were down and they held on to one another, just as they had on the day they had been taken away. Just before they disappeared inside, Frau Wagner turned to gaze at the black car as it revved its motor and pulled away from the curb. The appearance of her face startled Paul; she looked as if she had aged years in the days she had been away. Her cheeks sagged, her skin looked like worn leather, and her eyes were swollen.

Between Ernst's unwanted attention and the sight of his parents coming home, Paul craved some time to himself in a peaceful place. That weekend, he got on his bicycle and rode back to the beach at Lake Kaarst where he'd kissed Analia. He found the spot they had shared, sat down close to the lake's edge, and began to throw stones into the water.

The heat of the summer had disappeared weeks earlier, replaced with an early fall that made the day cool and slightly damp. Clouds covered the sky and gusts of wind cut through Paul's jacket to his skin. Despite the cool air, it felt comfortable to be here again: the clean air, the sound of gentle waves lapping against the sand, gulls squawking above his head. Paul could breathe here.

At the far end of the beach, a group of young people were gathered, the only other people to be seen. There were ten boys and girls about his age sitting in a circle. The sound of their laughter reached across the beach.

A pang of envy rose inside of him as he turned to watch. Those kids seemed so relaxed and at ease, not at all like what Paul had been feeling in the last weeks. They reminded him of a different time, a time when he would have met up with his friends on a weekend like this one, or maybe gone to the movies with a pal or two. Paul hadn't been to a movie in months. It wasn't that he couldn't still go; he could, though all movie theaters were off-limits to Jews. It's just that Paul hated that every movie these days began with a long newsreel glorifying Adolf Hitler. In the clips, crowds of people lined the streets to await his appearance. They shouted his name, screamed Nazi slogans, and even sobbed as if he were a famous movie star and they were his adoring fans. Paul detested it all. It seemed as if he could never get away from seeing Hitler's face; in school portraits, at youth rallies, in movie theaters, and on posters everywhere.

The kids across the beach started to sing. Their voices carried over to Paul who listened to the words in their song in stunned amazement.

The power of Hitler makes us small
We still lie bound and chained
But one day we will be free again
No more to be restrained!

To Paul's amazement, the song was about being free of Hitler. It suggested some kind of rebellion to end the oppression. Everyone knew that it was against the law to even think those things, let alone sing them out loud. Along with everything else, the Nazis had banned music that they called immoral or harmful. This included all music written by a Jewish composer or performed by a Jewish artist. It also included music like "western" jazz, which the Nazis considered offensive because it was associated with their enemies. But this song—talking about being free of Hitler—that would be considered evil and treasonous.

Who were these kids? Paul rose, brushed the sand from his jacket, and crossed the beach toward the group of young people. The closer he got, the louder the song became. *One day we will be free again, no more to be restricted!* The refrain echoed in Paul's ears.

He was just about to reach the group when his path was suddenly blocked by a young girl. She wore a long colorful skirt and a brown jacket over her white blouse. Startled, Paul stopped in his tracks as the girl eyed him, up and down. Her eyes were wary and distrustful. Paul stared back. He thought that he knew her, or recognized her from school.

"Is there something you want?" she asked, hands stuffed into her jacket pockets, feet spread apart on the sand.

"I was just curious," he replied.

"Curious or nosey? There's a difference."

The girl had long blond braids, deep blue eyes, and a burning stare that went right through Paul. He tried not to squirm.

"I just want to see who is singing," Paul said, gesturing toward the group. He took a step to get around the girl, but she blocked his way once more.

"I need to find out who you are before you go any further."

"Are you their guard?" Paul asked. This girl seemed tough; he liked that.

"Who are you?" she asked. "What's your name?"

"Paul. Paul Ritter." He had nothing to hide from her.

"What are you doing here?"

"I just came to the beach, to get away…from things."

She still looked wary. Paul understood that look of suspicion. Everyone had their guard up these days. Friend or foe? Who would turn you in for anything?

"I think I recognize you," Paul tried again. "We go to the same school."

The girl's eyes narrowed. "There are a lot of people who go to my school. That doesn't mean much."

"But I've seen you there—in the hallway. I don't think we're in the same grade, but I'm sure you've seen me, too."

The girl did not reply.

"Look, I really am just curious. I'm not going to do anything to you or your friends." Paul gestured toward the rest of the group. "You can trust me."

"Hard to know who to trust these days."

The song that the young people were singing continued in the background, their voices rising and falling. Paul tried to talk again. "That song…."

"What about it?"

"It's…it's fantastic! The best thing I've heard in a long time."

That was when the look in the girl's eyes began to change. Suspicion had turned into interest. Her face relaxed, her shoulders fell from around her ears, and a small smile began to tug at the corners of her mouth.

"I mean it!" Paul added.

"It's a protest song," the girl said.

Protest was something that Paul had been searching for, a way to stand up and fight back.

"We sing it all the time."

"But how?" Paul asked. "How can you sing those things? I mean, aren't you afraid that they'll hear you? The Nazis?"

The girl flung a braid off her shoulder and raised her chin into the air. "So, what if they do?"

Paul knew the answer to that. Surely, this girl knew as well. She and the members of her group could be arrested, thrown in jail, possibly hanged! But she didn't seem to care—or at least she didn't show it. Paul dug his foot into the sand and lowered his head. The sun was just starting to go down on the horizon. The air had grown cooler and the wind was picking up, pushing the sand into small dunes and hills. The colors in the sky had changed from cloudy gray to deep pink and blue.

"Aren't you afraid you'll get into trouble?"

The girl laughed. "Our cause is bigger than our fear!"

Cause! What cause was she talking about? By now, Paul's curiosity about this group was piqued. There was so much more that he wanted to know.

"It must be nice to feel as if you have a voice," he

finally said. Paul felt as if his own voice had disappeared. He wanted to scream, to protest and renounce everything that the Nazis stood for. Instead, he played the game of going along with them in order not to endanger himself and his family. This girl might not be afraid, but Paul certainly was.

"I'm Erika."

Paul lifted his head and stared at her. She was smiling now, and any hint of mistrust had disappeared.

"But everyone calls me Kiki." The singing in the background was dying down, the last notes trailing away. "Come on," she said. "I'll introduce you to some of the others."

CHAPTER 8

Paul eagerly followed Kiki as she turned and led him toward the group of young people.

"This is Paul Ritter," she announced. "He wanted to meet us. He liked the song," she added.

With that, she began to introduce Paul around the group. He grasped outstretched hands and shook them as the names flew by him. Elias, Luka, Charlotte. Some of the young people identified themselves with nicknames; a red-haired girl named Cherry, a rather large boy who called himself Biggie, a smiling girl named Sunshine, and so on. No one seemed particularly worried about his being here. He assumed that Kiki, as the lookout, was the one to determine who might be trusted and allowed to come in, and who needed to be kept away. He figured that he had passed the test. Besides, if anything went wrong, he'd be easily outnumbered.

Introductions finished, Paul was invited to sit down in the circle and join them. He sank down onto the sand and looked around. A number of the boys had hair cropped as short as his. He thought he recognized a couple of them from his Hitler Youth group. But Paul was startled to see that several of the boys had long, unruly hair falling below their ears, with bangs that flopped down over their eyes—just like his own hair had looked before he joined the Hitler Youth. How did these boys get away with that?

"So, you enjoyed our singing?" one of the older boys asked. Paul remembered his name was Luka and he was one of the boys with long hair. He wore a colorful checkered shirt and a leather cap that was perched on one side of his head. Kiki had introduced him as her brother, and he seemed to be the leader of the group.

Paul nodded. "I've never heard anything like it."

Luka laughed. "I imagine you haven't!"

"Those kinds of songs are forbidden in Germany. I'm sure you know that. I mean, I'm a member of the Hitler Youth. I have to be," Paul added quickly. "It's not that I want to. But if anyone in the group was caught singing something like that…." He didn't finish the sentence.

"I'm a member of the Hitler Youth, too," another boy, added. "So are a few of the others. And yes, we have been forced to join as well. When we're at a meeting, we raise our arm and salute Hitler and pledge our loyalty to him. But here, it's a different story."

"Who are you?" Paul asked.

"We're called the Edelweiss Pirates," Luka explained.

Paul frowned. What an odd name!

"It's because of this." Kiki reached up to the collar of her jacket and flipped it over. There was a small metal pin attached to the inside of her collar. On the face of the simple pin and engraved into the center was a white, multi-petaled flower.

"Do you know the Edelweiss flower?" she asked.

"It comes from Austria, doesn't it?"

She nodded. "Yes. These flowers are found in the mountains there, the Alps. They grow on the side of rocks and cliffs and stay alive in all kinds of weather, even snow." She gestured to the group. "That's kind of what we're like: persistent and strong. We survive, no matter what."

One by one, the members of the group flipped over the collar of their sweaters and jackets to reveal their Edelweiss pins.

"This is how we can tell who is a Pirate and who isn't," Kiki continued. "You show this pin, and we know that you're one of us, no questions asked."

"You mean there are more of you?" Paul's eyes swept the group.

Everyone laughed. "Oh, there are hundreds, maybe thousands of us," Kiki said.

She went on to explain that there were groups of Pirates in just about every city in Germany, and that they had been forming for several years, growing in number every day.

"We hate everything that Hitler stands for. He's trying to control not only what we do, but what we think. We won't let him do that."

Paul sat in stunned silence while Kiki continued talking. She said that some members of the group still went to school, while others had stopped attending.

"Some, like Luka," she pointed at her brother, "won't stand at attention for a Nazi flag. He refuses to be part of the Hitler Youth."

"The Nazis pull the strings and young boys jump up and down to please them," Luka said bitterly. "I won't do that."

"But how can you refuse?" Paul asked.

Luka's eyes hardened. "At first, I thought they were harmless and I went along with their rules—even signing up for the Hitler Youth. But then, my father was arrested." Luka went on to explain that his father had worked as a welder. He protested when a Jewish man who had also worked at the plant for years was fired. "And for that," Luka continued, "the Gestapo came to our house in the middle of the night and took my dad away. He barely had time to say good-bye." Luka's eyes burned with anger.

"Where did they take him?"

"Esterwegen concentration camp," Luka replied bitterly. "It's about two hundred and fifty kilometers north of here. He's been gone for three months. Three months for trying to stand up for a fellow worker who happened to be Jewish."

Paul swallowed hard. "Have you been able to visit him?"

Luka shook his head. "It's too far, and we have no way of knowing if we could see him even if we managed to get there. We have no idea when he'll be released. After he was arrested, I was done with the Nazis and the Hitler Youth. I moved out of our home and joined the Pirates."

Several of the other boys nodded and muttered their agreement.

"There are others in the group whose parents have also been arrested by the Nazis," Luka continued. "Now I camp in the woods with a few of those lads, or here on the beach, or sometimes in a farmer's barn when one lets us. We get food wherever we can. We manage."

Through all of this, Kiki sat with her head down, not saying a word. Now she raised it. "In all the time our dad's been gone, we've only gotten one letter from him. From the little we know of Esterwegen, it sounds pretty bad—hardly any food, back-breaking labor, and beatings if you're too weak to do the work. I was just as angry as Luka was when all this happened. But I knew I couldn't leave my mother alone. So, I still live at home and still go to school." She glanced at Paul. "And yes, I've seen you in the hallway."

"Kiki's a good daughter," Luka said, looking admiringly at his sister. "I'm grateful she stays with our mother."

"I'm a member of the League of German Girls," Kiki added.

That was the female branch of the Hitler Youth. The girls underwent physical training that included long hours of marching and hiking, just like the boys. Hitler wanted young German girls to be strong and fit, even though they weren't being groomed to be soldiers.

"Instead, they want us to be good wives and mothers one day," Kiki said, smiling grimly. "With those 'good' Nazi values that we're going to pass on to our children."

Luka chuckled. "You'll show them!"

"And it's okay with you that some of you belong to those Nazi groups and others don't?" Paul asked.

Kiki shrugged. "You do what you need to do to survive. What's important is that we all agree to resist, no matter where we live or where we have to belong. Each one of us is doing our part to stop Hitler."

Stop him? It's what Paul wanted as well. But how was

that possible? Each day, the newspapers were filled with articles and photographs celebrating Hitler's growing power. Just the other day, one newspaper had reported that the armament factory in Düsseldorf was cranking out military machinery at a frantic pace. Another photo showed scores of new fighter planes and Nazi tanks, all designed to demonstrate the might of Adolf Hitler. And then there were all the laws and rules against Jews. Those, too, were growing on a daily basis.

"I don't think you're going to be able to stop Hitler," Paul finally said, shaking his head. "None of you are strong enough to do that."

Luka eyed him carefully. "It's not that we're a fighting army. We're not going to stop him that way. But there are other kinds of resistance. Our mission is to find those other ways."

The sun was just about to disappear on the horizon. The air had turned cold and a light rain was beginning to fall. Paul needed to leave. His parents would be worried about where he was, and riding home from the beach in the dark would be difficult. He rose and said his good-byes to the group. But before leaving, he faced them once more.

"I want to know more about the Edelweiss Pirates," he said.

Kiki smiled. "We usually don't sit out on the beach like this. Today, it was deserted, so we gathered here.

Our usual campsite is way down there, through the woods, and about fifty paces to a clearing." She pointed to a patch of trees with a small gap between two large bushes. Then she looked back at Paul. "Come back some other time. We'll be right over there."

CHAPTER 9

Tuesday, September 20, 1938

Paul thought about what Kiki and the Edelweiss Pirates had said through that night and for the next couple of days.

Hitler is trying to control not only what we do but what we think.

Each one of us is doing our part to stop him.

There are many kinds of resistance.

All those things echoed what Paul had been thinking and struggling with. But what could he do? He couldn't get the Edelweiss Pirates out of his head. He was so pre-occupied during his meals with his parents, his mother thought he might be getting sick.

"Do I need to check your temperature?" she asked as Paul sat at breakfast, staring absently into space. "You haven't been eating. And you look as if you're a million miles away. What's wrong? Tell me."

Paul shook his head. "I'm fine, Mama. It's nothing. Really!" He trained his eyes evenly on his mother.

"I know it disturbs you to go to those Hitler Youth meetings," Mama continued. "You really should talk more about what goes on there. It helps to get it out."

His mother had continued to question him after every meeting. At first, he had complied, but lately he had pulled back. He just couldn't talk about it. It was bad enough to live the experience, but to *relive* it was becoming torture.

His father cleared his throat. "It must have been good to get to the beach the other day."

Paul looked up startled. "Why are you mentioning that?"

"No reason," his father replied, brow creased. The dimple in his cheek deepened. "I just know how much you love the beach. And you came home so late that night. I just assumed it was a good day for you."

Paul swallowed hard. "Yes, it was a great day."

His parents exchanged uneasy glances but didn't say another word.

There was another Hitler Youth meeting that afternoon. For some unknown reason, the boys had been told to meet at a spot next to the market on Carlsplatz, rather than at the fairground. Paul hadn't wandered through the market on the way home from school in weeks. It just didn't seem to have the same appeal as it once had. Now, he walked to the meeting point with Harold by his side. It was Harold's first time back since his injury.

"How are you feeling?" Paul asked. "Your leg?"

"It's better, I guess."

A thin strip of gauze held down with tape still covered the wound on Harold's leg, evidence that the injury had not healed completely. But more than that, Harold still looked jumpy and scared, as though the inside of him was not yet healed either.

Up ahead, Paul could already hear Franz on his megaphone blasting out an order for the boys to assemble in lines. Paul looked over at Harold. "You're the one who talked me into joining. Are you still so sure it was a good idea?"

Harold's face looked grim. "What choice do we have?"

Franz wasted no time in announcing that the boys would be going on a special mission that day.

"I'm not going to say too much about it now," he boomed through his speaker. "Just know that you will be serving our great Führer through your actions."

The excitement in Franz's voice unnerved Paul. Serving Hitler was not what he wanted to do. This special mission, whatever it was, could not be good. But Franz was not giving anything away. Without another word, everyone lined up and began to march in quick pace away from the market and east to the Königsallee, the one-kilometer boulevard that ran through the busiest part of the city. It was a wide avenue lined on either side with shops and cafés. The Düsseldorf opera house was there along with several theaters. The entire boulevard was cut in half by a lazy flowing canal—a tributary of the Rhine river. One side of the avenue was joined to the other by two iron bridges that allowed foot traffic and cars to cross. Chestnut trees dotted the stone walkway by the river's edge, along with several fountains that spewed water high into the air. At night, the fountains were lit up.

Franz raised his hand to slow the marching boys. Up ahead, Paul could just make out a group of people who had already gathered in a clump. He couldn't see much and didn't know who they were. But the uneasy feeling he had had when Franz first announced this mystery mission was still there and getting stronger by the minute.

"Do you know what we're doing here?" he whispered to Harold who shook his head in reply. Harold looked as anxious as Paul felt.

"We're here to put the Jews to work."

Paul spun around to face Ernst who had come up behind him.

"What are you talking about?" Paul asked.

"I overheard Franz and some of the other older boys. The police have ordered that a group of Jews come out and clean the streets of Düsseldorf. We're here to supervise them."

"But why are Jews cleaning the streets?" Paul still didn't understand.

Ernst snorted. "You'll find out."

Just then, Franz gave a command to move forward. The boys marched, slower this time, toward the clump of people. Paul still couldn't see a thing. And then, as if on cue, the group ahead suddenly parted open and the sight that greeted Paul made his stomach tighten. A group of Jewish people—men, women, old, young— were on their hands and knees on the pavement. Gray pails dotted the sidewalk in front of them. Each person had a brush in hand and was scrubbing the pavement, methodically moving the brush up and down and around in circles. With rising dread, Paul recognized the teller that his father used to speak to on his weekly runs to the bank, along with one of the doctors that had worked at his mother's hospital. There were probably other doctors in the group, Paul thought, along with lawyers, teachers, shopkeepers, and housewives. Not that any of these people were working any longer; Jews had been banned from most jobs. But the people in front of him on their hands and knees were dressed like any other citizen of Düsseldorf. They were dressed as if they were going to work. But instead, they were on the ground, forced to do this demeaning labor.

Other citizens of Düsseldorf stood in a wide circle, gawking at the Jews as if they were animals in a circus display. Once in a while, Paul heard hecklers in the crowd shout out: "You're not wanted here! Send them away! Get rid of the Jews!" Others thrust their angry fists in the air and shouted their approval.

Franz raised his hand and brought the boys to a halt. He turned to face them. "Take positions around the Jews," he shouted. "Make sure they are washing every square inch of the pavement. Report any problems to me."

This can't be happening! Paul's brain was on fire. He felt sick to his stomach. He needed to run away, escape, hide! But he had to do as he was told or there would be even more trouble for him. His eyes darted in wild circles trying to figure out what to do and where to stand. He finally picked a spot behind some of the other boys where he couldn't see the faces of the people kneeling in front of him. Maybe, if he couldn't see their humiliation, he could pretend it wasn't as bad as it really was. At least, that's what he was trying to talk himself into believing. Harold managed to find a place next to him.

"What should we do?" Harold whispered. His face looked gray. His eyes were as wide open as they could possibly stretch.

Paul was just about to tell him to keep his head down and try not to be seen, when suddenly someone cried out. Paul peered around the shoulder of the boy in front of him and saw that an elderly Jewish man had faltered while trying to get onto his hands and knees. The hat he wore on his head had fallen to the ground, unleashing a mop of white hair. The man was sprawled out on the pavement, struggling. Without thinking, Paul pushed in front of the boy blocking him. He was just about to reach out and help the man up, when suddenly Franz appeared.

"Get on your knees!" Franz shouted at the man. His face smoldered with complete hatred. The elderly man was still struggling. Paul didn't know what to do. He longed to reach out to the man but was terrified at the same time.

"I said, on your knees!" Franz's voice was high and tight. This time, the man cringed and covered his head with his arms.

"I'll teach you not to ignore me," Franz yelled a third time as he lifted his arm, ready to strike.

"Troop leader!" Paul shouted out.

Franz paused and turned. His face was still dark, his eyes still threatening.

"I'm…I'm sorry, troop leader," Paul stuttered. He swallowed hard, his throat as dry as dust. "But some of the boys down the line need your help to get themselves organized. They're crowding each other and don't know what to do." It was the only thing he could think of to say.

Franz, arm still in the air, turned slightly to look down the sidewalk. Sure enough, several Hitler Youth boys were standing in a cluster, jostling one another. It was just the distraction that Paul had hoped for.

"You boys!" Franz bellowed at the group. "I told you to supervise the Jews. Stop standing there doing nothing and do your job." With that, he dropped his arm and marched toward the boys.

Paul exhaled the breath that he had been holding. When he turned back to the elderly man, he saw that another woman next to him had already helped him to a kneeling position. Paul was just about to move back and disappear behind the other boys again when a girl at the far end of the row of Jews raised her head. Paul sucked in his breath once more as their eyes met. It was Analia. She was there, kneeling on the ground, scrubbing the pavement. Her mother and father were next to her. Her eyes met Paul's and stared.

Analia's face was pale and thin. Her hair fell limply over her shoulders. Her clothes were shabby and hung on her body as if she had not eaten well in a long time. A yellow Star of David was sewn onto the lapel of her jacket. But it was her eyes that haunted Paul. Her eyes were pleading with him—begging him for help.

His heart began to hammer in his chest as he stared back at her. He longed to run to her, talk to her, reassure her—anything! His mind struggled in this tug of war: wanting to go to her yet needing to stay put. And as they stared at each other, Analia's eyes turned from pleading to fearful as she suddenly took note of his Hitler Youth uniform.

Paul's mind screamed out *NO!* He needed to tell her that the uniform meant nothing, that he hated everything about it and about the group that he had been forced to join. He needed to tell her that he was on her side, that he was still her friend. But once again, he felt powerless to do anything.

And as he watched, helplessly, Analia's face began to harden into a look of defiance, anger, then hatred. Her eyes narrowed and she raised her chin and flipped her hair off her shoulder. She turned away, bent down, and began to scrub the pavement once more.

CHAPTER 10
Sunday, September 25, 1938

The look in Analia's eyes haunted Paul for days. And even more than that, he was plagued by his own failure to help her. *Analia must think I'm the enemy*, he thought, furious at himself for not having done anything! *I could have spoken to her. I could have gone over to her, pretended I was there to supervise her, and then whispered some kind of message.* Instead, he had done nothing.

That weekend, Paul returned to the beach. He hadn't stopped thinking about the Edelweiss Pirates since he had met them a week ago. And after having witnessed the Jewish citizens of Düsseldorf being made to clean the pavement, he thought about the Pirates more and more. He still didn't really know what it was that they did. They had talked about resistance, but what did that really mean? Maybe they could do something to help Analia and the others. Maybe there was something he could do with them.

The beach was deserted when Paul arrived. And it was quiet. There was only the sound of several gulls that squawked near the edge of the lake, fighting over a small fish. Paul stowed his bike behind a tree. Then, following Kiki's instructions, he walked to the far end of the beach to the clump of trees she had pointed out. It was hard at first to find the two large bushes with the small gap between them. He tried several spots until he finally parted the branches of two larger bushes and saw the footpath behind. The light from the beach was swallowed up as Paul walked into the woods following the path. Outgrown roots, wildflowers, small sticks, and fallen leaves crunched under his feet as he walked fifty paces in, silently counting each step. He waved away a couple of mosquitos that buzzed around his face. He pushed aside a branch that was blocking the path and jumped over a fallen tree trunk. Finally, up ahead, he saw a young boy whom he recognized from the last time—the new sentry, Paul guessed. He approached the boy who looked at Paul and let him pass with a brief nod of his head.

Paul saw the group gathered around a small fire dug deep into the ground. Several Pirates were feeding it sticks and branches from a pile that sat next to the pit.

Others were lying on the ground, leaning against logs, chatting easily with one another. Three small canvas tents were pitched in a circle behind the fire. Paul figured they were for Luka and the others who lived apart from their families. A girl was singing another protest song, strumming on a guitar. It was a song Paul hadn't heard before.

> *Hitler's power may lay us low*
> *And keep us locked in chains,*
> *But we will smash the chains one day,*
> *We'll be free again.*

Kiki was there in the middle of the pack, and Paul made a beeline to talk to her. No one stopped him or got in his way.

"I want to join up!" Paul blurted out. The words came as a bit of a surprise even to his ears. Yes, he wanted to do something to help, but was he really prepared to join this group he knew very little about, and participate in dangerous activities against the Nazis? The answer was simple, after today: Of course he was. For him, there was no longer another choice. Paul stood in front of Kiki, shivering slightly in the cool September air. He shoved his hands into his pockets. The fire next to him did nothing to stop the trembling.

Kiki sized Paul up from head to toe just as she had done when he had first approached the group a week earlier. And then she asked, "What made you decide?"

He told her about having to supervise the Jews as they cleaned the streets. He talked about the old man who had fallen and wasn't able to get up, and Franz who had very nearly beaten him. And he told her about Analia and the look of anger in her eyes when she saw his Hitler Youth uniform. "She's my friend. She was forced to get on her knees and clean the pavement," he said. "And I did nothing to help her."

Kiki sighed and hung her head. "We hate what Hitler is doing to the Jews. It's one of the most shameful things. We've helped some Jewish families who have been trying to find a safer place to live. Luka hid a family at this campsite until we figured out a better plan for them."

"I need to find a way to do something for my friend," Paul said. "Joining the Pirates is the answer I've been looking for."

"And what about the Hitler Youth?"

Paul looked down and then back up at Kiki. "I have to stay in. I won't move away from my family. And the only way to keep my parents and myself safe is to pretend I'm one of them. That's what you and some of the others have been doing, isn't it?"

The chatter around Paul and Kiki had faded. Luka and the others were listening to their conversation. It was completely quiet in the woods except for the crackle of logs on the fire and screeching birds that flew high above the trees. Finally, Luka approached Paul. He pulled his leather cap off his head and held out his hand.

"Glad to know you want to be one of us."

Startled, Paul accepted the outstretched hand and shook it. "Is that it? I'm an Edelweiss Pirate?"

Luka shook his head. "I'm afraid it's not quite that simple."

Paul pulled his hand back. "Why not?"

"Well, we need to see how serious you are about all of this."

"I'm serious," Paul insisted. "I told you all the reasons I want to join."

"And they're good ones," Luka replied, replacing his cap. "But we still have to see you in action. Think of it as a kind of test."

A test! Paul wasn't sure what that meant and didn't like the sound of it. The test to be part of the Hitler Youth had meant jumping a dangerous firepit. Surely, this group wasn't going to make him do something like that! He breathed in and out and looked Luka straight in the eyes. "Okay, tell me what I have to do."

That was when Kiki joined in again. She smiled at Paul. "Wait for our signal. You'll find out when the time is right."

CHAPTER 11

Friday, September 30, 1938

Days went by. Paul returned to school and waited. He went back to the Hitler Youth meetings where Franz boasted about how they had put the Jews to work and how there would be many more glorious opportunities to do that sort of thing again. That was the word he used to describe it: *herrlich*, glorious!

And still Paul waited. He heard nothing from the Pirates about what they might be planning and how he might be involved. He heard nothing about whether or not they were going to accept him into the group. Every now and then, he passed Kiki in the hallway of his school building. He glanced at her, eager to see if she had any news for him. But she treated him like a complete stranger, pushing past him without a second look. He was beginning to think that the Pirates had misled him—that they were all talk and no action—that it was a fantasy to think he would ever be able to stand up to the injustices that Hitler had created. And then one day, Kiki passed him in the hallway once more. This time, instead of ignoring him, she caught his eye. It was so subtle that Paul nearly missed it. But as he got close to her, he noticed that she had raised an eyebrow ever so slightly. And as he was about to pass, she flipped over the collar of her blouse and flashed her Edelweiss pin. It happened in a split second. And then she was gone, walking quickly through the hallway to her class.

The pin! It was the signal that Kiki had told him about. Paul could barely focus for the rest of the day. Aside from the pounding in his chest that he thought everyone would be able to hear, he still had questions. What were the Pirates going to do? What was *he* going to do? How was this all going to happen? Would he pass whatever test they had in mind?

At the end of the day, he was just about to stuff his books into his bookbag when he noticed a small piece of paper in one corner of the bag that hadn't been there before. Paul rolled it open and read the scrawled message: *Under the iron bridge on Königsallee, 9:00 p.m.*

The blood drained from his face. Who had put this in his bag? And when? He shoved the note back inside and glanced around. Most of his classmates had already left. Harold hadn't been there that day; he was home nursing a cold. Paul bolted out the door and headed home. He barely said hello to his parents. He grabbed a slice of buttered bread and disappeared into his bedroom, calling out that he had a lot of homework to do and probably wouldn't join them for dinner. The truth was he was too nervous to eat a meal and was afraid that if he sat with his parents at the dinner table, they would ask about his lack of appetite and he might crumble under their questioning. He couldn't risk it. Instead, he paced nervously in his room until it became dark. Then, he dressed in a black shirt and pants and grabbed his jacket. He caught a glimpse of himself in a mirror before leaving his bedroom. His face was flushed. Taking a deep breath, he steadied himself, and walked out.

His parents didn't question him when he said he was going over to Harold's house, explaining that his friend had been sick that day and he wanted to go over some schoolwork with him. At least the part about Harold being sick was true! He walked quickly toward the center of town and arrived at the first bridge on Königsallee before the clock tower at the central train station chimed nine bells. He was early and at first couldn't see anyone else there. He stood by the bridge, looking around. This was so close to the spot where, days earlier, Analia and the other Jews had been made to scrub the pavement.

He thought about that when he suddenly heard someone whisper his name. Whirling around, he saw Kiki in the shadows, standing under an archway of the bridge.

"I thought you might be here early, so I came to keep you company until the others arrive." She motioned him to join her. "Get out of the light where someone might see you."

Paul quickly moved toward Kiki and followed her under the bridge and into a darkened walkway, hidden from view. She took a sharp turn and together they emerged into an unfinished chamber. Paul was surprised to see a stockpile of supplies spread on the stone floor: ropes, backpacks, and cans of food.

"We're not sure why this room is here," Kiki said. "Maybe the builders who constructed the bridge built this space for the workers. Luka found this place when he was scouting for somewhere to meet up when we're planning something in the city. It's easier than being at the beach and then having to get into town, and it's completely hidden away, so the Nazi police don't know we're here. We call this place our bunker." She pointed to several cots lined up in a corner. "Luka and a few of the others sometimes sleep here when they can't get back to the campsite."

Paul surveyed the space. It was cool and damp. Small droplets of water trickled down the wall in several places.

A guitar sat in a corner, along with a wooden chair that held some jackets and shirts. Pillows and wool blankets were thrown across the cots. A small shelf, broken on one end, held a few books, along with a couple of plates, knives, and forks. The only light came from a small opening—really just a break in the brick wall. Rays of milky moonlight shone through the room. Paul shivered.

"It's not ideal," Kiki said, reading his mind. "But it's safe."

Like Paul, Kiki was dressed in black. Even her long, blond braids were hidden under a dark cap. She eyed him up and down. "You look nervous."

"I am." There was no point in lying to her.

"I've been doing this for some time. You get used to the nerves after a while. But they never go away. Nerves are a good thing," she added. "They keep you sharp."

"How long? I mean, how long have you been a Pirate?"

She paused. "About a year. I think I was one of the youngest to join the group. My brother was already a Pirate. When I realized what he was doing, I knew I had to be part of it. I knew I had to join."

"Does your mother know anything about this?"

She shook her head. "About me? No. She figured out that Luka was doing something that was against the law, especially when he quit the Hitler Youth. She never wanted him to quit, even after our father was arrested. You can't imagine the fights that went on in our house when Luka stopped going to meetings. She was afraid he'd be taken away as well. Our mother would be sick with worry if she knew I was part of this. I have to hide it from her."

"This has split your family apart," Paul said.

"Yes. Splitting up the family is terrible. But it's been necessary for the cause."

"I know you said you didn't want to leave your mother alone after Luka left. But doesn't it tear you apart to be living a lie?" Paul asked. "Staying at home and following Nazi rules." It was exactly what he was feeling.

Kiki sighed. "It's complicated. In my heart, all I want to do is to be part of the resistance. But our father is gone. And my mother has lost Luka. It would break her heart to lose me as well. So, I stay. And I pretend."

"I'm not saying a word to my parents about any of this," Paul said. "I think it's safer that way. They've never approved of Hitler. In fact, they hate everything he stands for. But they would be sick with worry if they knew what I was doing, what I am about to do."

"You have to believe that they'd be proud of you. I believe that my father would think that. And my mother, if she really understood it all. It's what helps get me through."

A few more members of the group were arriving at the bridge. Luka was there and quickly assembled everyone into a circle. He looked at Paul.

"Good to see you here," he said.

Paul smiled, trying to stop the nervous twitch in his upper lip. But if Luka noticed, he didn't say a word.

"You all know what you need to do," Luka said, addressing the group. "And you'll pick it up in no time," he added to Paul. Then, he motioned for the group to follow him. Keeping their heads low, they crept out of the shadows of the bridge and toward the main boulevard until they were standing by a large building, directly in front of the spot where Analia and the others had been ordered to clean the pavement. A couple of the Pirates were placed on guard duty, there to alert the group if anyone came near or there was trouble of any kind. Several of the Pirates carried tin pails, much like the ones that had been placed on the pavement in front of the Jews that day, except that these pails contained white paint. The Pirates also held paintbrushes in their hands. Paul watched as Kiki and the others approached the wall of the building beside the pavement. They dipped their brushes into the pails and began to smear the wall with thick brushstrokes. When Kiki stood back a minute later, Paul read what she had painted: *Hitler will not win!* Then, Luka handed a tin pail and brush to

Paul. "Your turn to tell the Nazis what you really think of them," he said.

Adrenaline coursed through Paul's body. His heart hammered in his chest, the feeling rising up into his ears. His breath was rapid and shallow. *This is it*, he thought. *My first act of resistance.* If he and the others were caught, who knew what might happen to them? But in this moment, Paul didn't care. He walked up to the wall, dipped the brush in the pail, and began to draw big, fat, white letters. He wrote: *Down with Hitler!*

The group worked for a long time, adding more paint to the wall until it was dotted with messages: *Resist the Nazis! Victory! Freedom for the Jews!* At one point, Kiki looked over at Paul and smiled, giving him a big thumbs-up. Paul grinned back.

When they had finished covering the wall with painted slogans, the pirates gathered up their paint cans and brushes and headed back to the bunker. Once they were huddled inside, Luka came up to Paul.

"You did well," he said, extending his hand as he had done in the forest. "You're an Edelweiss Pirate now."

Startled, Paul said, "That's it? That was the test?" It had been almost too easy. "And now I'm one of you?"

"What do you want?" Luka asked. "A ceremony?"

The group around Paul broke out in laughter. And after a moment, Paul joined them. He hadn't laughed in such a long time and it felt good. It felt as if he was letting go of something, or maybe running toward something, a feeling of crossing the finish line at the end of a long race.

Kiki walked over to him. "Hold out your hand," she said.

She dropped something into it. And when Paul looked down, he saw that there was an Edelweiss pin resting in his palm. The metal rim caught the ray of moonlight that seeped in through the small opening in the wall and glistened.

"You put this on and you're an Edelweiss Pirate," she said. "No turning back."

This is it, Paul thought. He took a deep breath and then attached the pin to the underside of his shirt collar, patting it in place and turning the collar back down to conceal it.

Kiki smiled approvingly. "Wear the pin when you're out with us on a mission. But make sure when you're not wearing it, that you keep it in a safe place," she added. "You wouldn't want anyone else to get hold of it."

All the nerves that had been surging through Paul's body were still there, he realized. But there was the added feeling of pure exhilaration. His cheeks glowed and his eyes sparkled as he thought of Analia. There was no question that a part of him was doing this for her. But he was also doing it for the old Jewish man who had very nearly been beaten, and for all the other

Jews who had been humiliated that day on the streets of Düsseldorf. And above all, he was doing this for himself, affirming his desire and responsibility to be a good and moral person, no matter what the risk. That was the best feeling of all.

CHAPTER 12

Saturday, October 1, 1938

Franz was fuming the next day at the Hitler Youth meeting.

"Someone wrote on the walls of our city and dishonored our country and our great leader," he bellowed into his megaphone. He described in great detail the graffiti that had been painted on the wall of the building in the center of town. Every time he mentioned a slogan that had been painted, the group of boys shouted "get them!" and "revenge!"

Paul kept his eyes forward the entire time, not wanting to look at Harold who was next to him, or worse, at Ernst who might detect something in his expression. He couldn't give anything away.

Franz went on to rant about what was going to

happen to the vandals when they were caught. "And trust me," he yelled. "They will be caught!" He urged anyone who knew or had seen or heard anything about the incident to report it to him. "It's your duty to reveal the enemies among us," he said.

The boys shouted their reply. "Yes, troop leader!"

The meeting couldn't end fast enough for Paul. When they were finally dismissed, he headed for his bicycle, hoping that he and Harold could bike home without having to talk. But just as they were about to push off, Paul was stopped by Ernst.

"Walk with me for a bit, Ritter," Ernst said.

Paul should have said that his parents needed him at home as soon as possible. But in that moment, an excuse failed him. Reluctantly, he got off his bike, and began to walk next to Ernst. Harold lagged a couple of steps behind.

Ernst wanted to talk about the graffiti and revenge. "If we find whoever vandalized the walls, who knows what will happen to them. You heard the troop leader. They'll probably be arrested or maybe shot. And they will deserve whatever they get." He turned around to call out to Harold. "What do you think about what happened, Becker?"

Harold had been quietly pushing his bike, his face turned down to the road. Now, he looked up at Ernst, but didn't answer. Harold had changed so much in the months since he had boasted about the Hitler Youth and wanted Paul to join. The injury to his leg after jumping the fire, not to mention seeing Ernst's parents taken away, and being forced to supervise the Jews on the street, had shut him down. Not even Paul could get much out of him. And when Paul pressed Harold to say something, his only reply was, "None of this is what I thought it was going to be."

Ernst snorted. "Do you have an opinion, Becker, or are you just going to say nothing, as usual?"

Still no reply from Harold. So, Ernst turned back to Paul. "You're awfully quiet as well. Don't you agree with me? Shouldn't we punish the traitors?"

Paul knew he had to play along with the ruse that he supported the Hitler Youth. Still, he wanted to speak up. He wanted to confront Ernst and challenge his beliefs. There had to be something that he could say.

"It was probably just some kids up to tricks," Paul said carefully. "I'm sure they meant no harm."

Ernst's mouth dropped open. "No harm? They wrote 'Down with Hitler!' That's an act of treason." Ernst stared at him, eyes narrowing. "You're not sympathizing with anyone who would challenge our great leader, are you?"

"No, of course not," Paul replied, even more cautiously. "I'm just saying that we don't know anything about the ones who did this."

Ernst's stare rested on Paul until he felt the sweat gather across his forehead. "Just watch what you say, Ritter," Ernst finally said. With that, he threw his leg over his bicycle and rode away.

Paul took a shaky breath and waited for Harold to catch up with him. The two walked in silence until they were close to their homes.

"Be careful, Paul," Harold said before turning up the block to his house. "You were right about Ernst. He can't be trusted."

CHAPTER 13

Wednesday, October 19, 1938

Paul buried his Edelweiss pin in the top drawer of his desk, underneath a pile of papers and notebooks. He knew it would be safe there. His parents rarely went into his room and never looked through his private things.

A couple of weeks later, he fished out the pin from his desk drawer and attached it to the underside of his jacket collar as he left his home for another mission with the Pirates. He had been on several other missions since they had painted the graffiti. One night, the group raided a food warehouse. They stole potatoes and cabbages and apples, distributing the food to Jewish families who were banned from shopping in most stores. Stores had big signs in their windows forbidding entry to Jews.

After the raid, Paul decided to drop off some food at Analia's home. He had continued to cycle by her apartment building over the weeks. Each time, he was sure that he saw the curtain move ever so slightly when he paused in front of the house. Ever since Analia had seen him in his Hitler Youth uniform, he was convinced that she wanted nothing to do with him. But each time he saw the curtain move, he believed that she and her family must still be in their home. This meant that they hadn't been shipped off to one of those terrible concentration camps.

It was dusk when he rode up to her building with a box of food. He stopped, got off his bike, and checked to make sure no one was watching. Then he walked up the path to the front door and placed the carton of food on her doorstep. He moved over to the window of her flat and knocked loudly on the glass. Then, he made a quick getaway, hiding behind a nearby tree.

Analia was the one who cautiously came to the front door of the building, opened it, and peeked outside. Paul caught his breath at the sight of her looking so pale and worn-down. She glanced down, saw the box, and bent to peer tentatively inside of it. When she saw the supplies, she lifted her head, her eyes darting up and down the street. Paul shrank further behind the tree and then looked carefully once more around its trunk. Analia picked up the box and closed the door with a soft click. Paul climbed back on his bike and rode away, both satisfied and sad. Analia would probably never know that he had left the food. Still, he was content that he had done something for her. In fact, each activity with the Pirates filled Paul with more and more pride. And each mission made his participation in the Hitler Youth just a bit easier to bear.

On this night, the group gathered under the bridge in their bunker, preparing to make a pamphlet drop at the new central train station. The plan was to leave piles of pamphlets at every entrance of the station for passengers to pick up the next morning. Someone had introduced Luka to a man with a small print shop in his basement. Usually, he printed newsletters for churches in the area. But he had agreed to produce flyers for the Pirates, no questions asked.

"He knows it's illegal and dangerous," Luka said. "But he's willing to help us. It just goes to show that there are still good people around. You just need to know where to look for them."

The man had generated hundreds of pamphlets with several different messages. One read: *Hitler and his followers will rob you of your rights, step by step, until one day nothing will be left but a system presided over by criminals.*

Another simply read: *Let Freedom Live!*

The one that Paul liked best stated: *The German people look the other way while Jews are being oppressed and murdered. Do not let this happen!*

Paul feared that Hitler's influence and power were reaching further across Europe and even across the ocean. Just a few days ago, his father had told him that Winston Churchill had given a speech where he warned that Hitler would soon start a war that would involve many countries including England. He advised Great Britain and even the United States to arm themselves. Churchill was an important politician in England. Many people thought he would eventually become prime minister. But even he feared Hitler and what he might be capable of doing. Paul had also heard the reports that more Jewish families were being sent to concentration camps.

"So, how are you feeling about being one of us?" Kiki came up beside Paul while he was folding pamphlets and stuffing them into his backpack.

Paul paused and turned to her. She was becoming a good friend, someone he could really talk to. Now, he thought long and hard about her question before answering. "I'm proud of what we're doing," he finally said. "But I don't know if it's enough." He told Kiki about the news reports from England and other places. "Hitler is moving so fast, faster than I imagined. Sometimes I wonder if what we're doing really makes a difference."

"It does," Kiki insisted. "If we can change one person's mind, or if we can help one family, that's important enough."

Paul nodded. "I just wish we could do more. And I hate having to pretend I'm one of *them*. I hate staying silent when the Hitler Youth put Jews and others down."

"I get it," Kiki said. "And I feel the same way. But remember, it's the silence that's keeping you safe—that's allowing us to do our work. You're standing up to them without having to declare it out loud."

"I just wonder how long this will go on."

"Not forever. There will come a time when you'll be able to speak up and say what you think, a time when all of us will be able to do that."

Paul shook his head. "When?" It was hard to imagine a time when he'd be able to speak his mind.

"You'll know when the time is right. You'll know when to break the silence. For now, you do more good by pretending."

Paul chuckled and looked at Kiki. "You always know exactly what to say to me."

She jabbed him playfully in the arm. "That's my job, to remind you and everyone else why we're here."

Paul and the rest of the Pirates gathered up the last pamphlets, stuffed them into their packs, and headed for the central train station. The station was used by more than one hundred thousand people every day who passed by on their way to work or to neighboring cities like Duisburg, twenty minutes away, or Essen, thirty minutes north east. It had been built in the 1800s. But over time, it had become too small for the growing population of Düsseldorf, so it was redesigned in 1930. It now featured a notable clock tower that was chiming ten bells when the Pirates approached.

Paul buttoned his jacket and pulled his collar up to his ears. It was only the middle of October, but it was getting colder, especially in the evenings. Winter was just around the corner. When he exhaled, he could see his breath hanging in the air, and he wished he'd brought a scarf to wrap around his neck, or at least some gloves. Rubbing his hands together, he blew on them to try and warm them up.

Luka stopped the Pirates close to the train station and gave them the silent signal to divide up into pairs; one person would be the lookout, and the other would drop bundles of pamphlets. That was something they had planned in advance. Paul was paired with Kiki, which comforted him. She had been on these missions so many more times than he had and knew exactly what she was doing. They worked quickly and silently, walking the perimeter of the massive station and depositing a pile of pamphlets at every door and window. Kiki acted as sentry and Paul deposited the bundles. Even at this late hour, the station was still open, so the two of them retreated into the shadows whenever Kiki gave a signal, a low whistle, that a group of passengers was about to push through the doors. Once the passengers were out of the way and the coast was clear, Paul and Kiki moved out of the shadows and continued their work.

Paul lost track of time. He was focused on leaving as many pamphlets as possible at each door of the station. Finally, he dug into his backpack and realized that he was getting close to the bottom of the pile. One more door and one more drop and they would be done. Paul glanced at Kiki and she gave him a thumbs-up. The coast was clear. He reached into his backpack and pulled out the last bundle of pamphlets. Then he approached the building. But this time, instead of leaving the pamphlets in a pile, he decided to scatter them all around the door.

He didn't even hear Kiki's soft but urgent whistle. He was thinking about the passengers that would be arriving the next morning and reading the messages that were written on these pamphlets. What would they think? Would they celebrate this act of defiance and support it? Would they hate what was written here and want to find out who had done this? Probably some combination of both; those who supported Hitler and those who secretly wished he was gone. Paul was emptying the last pamphlets from his backpack when there was a sudden shout from behind.

"Stop! What are you doing?"

Paul froze and then whirled around. Two Hitler Youth were moving quickly toward him—their uniforms were unmistakable, even in the dark. Kiki was instantly by his side. "Run!" she hissed.

That was all it took. Paul shoved the remaining pamphlets into his pockets and bolted away from the building, Kiki at his heels.

From behind him, the Hitler Youth shouted again, this time louder. "I said stop! This instant!" Paul recognized the voice: *Ernst.*

Paul picked up his pace, drawing on all his strength and skill as a runner to move as fast as he could. He could hear Kiki panting to catch her breath behind him. They had to get away, but he wasn't going to leave her behind. He slowed slightly so she could catch up and when she was next to him, he grabbed her arm and pulled her along, practically lifting her off her feet. Just as they were about to turn a corner, Paul glanced over his shoulder just in time to see Ernst at the door of the station, bending over to pick up a pamphlet. Ernst looked up and peered into the dark.

Did he recognize me? That was the last thought Paul had before he and Kiki disappeared around the corner.

CHAPTER 14

Monday, October 24, 1938

Luka had been caught during the pamphlet drop! When Paul and Kiki returned to the bunker, several Pirates were already there with the terrible news.

"Hitler Youth were out on patrol and came at us out of nowhere." That's what Biggie said, the Pirate who was partnered with Luka to drop pamphlets. "Luka hung back to divert their attention so that I could get away. But they got him."

There was stunned silence in the bunker as the reality set in. Luka! Not just one of their own, but their leader!

"What's going to happen to him?" Paul asked. His own close encounter with Ernst was nearly forgotten.

"They'll take him to Gestapo headquarters," Kiki replied, her voice trembling.

"And then what?"

She shook her head. "If he's lucky, he'll be questioned and released in a few days."

And if he's not lucky? This thought raced through Paul's mind as he faced a silent Kiki.

There was nothing more that the Pirates could do that night. Kiki told Paul that tomorrow morning they would send scouts out to see what they could find out about Luka. But in the meantime, they all needed to disperse and head to their homes. It was decided that the Pirates would lay low for the next few days. After the pamphlet drop, the Nazi police or the Hitler Youth would likely be out in greater numbers, patrolling around major buildings and landmarks. It was better to suspend any resistance activities than to risk another arrest.

"I'll give you the signal when it's time to return to the beach," Kiki said before taking off.

"Try not to worry too much," Paul said to her before he left. "Luka's strong and smart. You know that better than anyone."

Kiki smiled and nodded. But Paul could see the confused and sad look in her eyes.

In the meantime, Paul had no choice but to return to school and go back to his Hitler Youth meetings where he watched to see if there was anything different in the way Ernst treated him. He couldn't see any changes.

Ernst ranted to Franz and everyone else about how he had "come within an inch of catching the criminals who had left the pamphlets behind." That was Ernst's version of the story. Paul practically laughed out loud. Ernst could boast all he wanted; he would never have caught up to Paul!

It was only Harold who seemed to sense some change in Paul's behavior. "What's wrong with you?" Harold asked at the end of one meeting. "You seem as jumpy as I feel."

Paul needed to check himself. If Harold thought he was jumpy, others might think that as well. It was dangerous to give away his feelings. But try as he might, it was nearly impossible to relax. He was desperate for news of Luka, anxious to know what was going to happen to him.

Two more days passed with no news and then, one afternoon, Paul passed Kiki in the school hallway. Her head was down, her eyes trained on the floor. At first, he made a move to walk around her. But then, she lifted her head, nodded at him, and flashed her Edelweiss pin from under her collar. Paul's heart raced. The rest of the day could not pass quickly enough.

At the end of the day, Paul muttered to Harold that he had to run some errands for his parents. Harold eyed him with some doubt, but Paul didn't stick around for questions. He jumped on his bike and headed straight for the campsite in the woods. It was cloudy and cold that afternoon, and the woods felt as if they were wrapped in a dark cloak. Up ahead at the campsite, Paul spotted a group of Pirates already gathered. And when he came closer, the group parted and there was Luka, sitting on the ground, leaning against a log with Kiki by his side.

Paul could not believe his eyes. Luka was back! He had returned to the Pirates. Paul's heart jumped and a smile spread across his face. But a moment later, he paused when he had a closer look. A deep cut, still raw and angry stood out above Luka's eyebrow. His lower lip was cracked and swollen, and his right eye was bruised and half-closed.

Paul had a million questions, but Luka wanted to wait until all the Pirates were assembled. Finally, when everyone was there, Luka quieted the group and began to talk.

"First of all, I'm fine," he began. "A little beat up, but fine."

Murmurs traveled across the group. Luka hushed everyone and continued.

"I might have gotten away from the train station if there had only been one or two Hitler Youth that jumped me. But there were three, and I had no chance. They dragged me to the old town and to the *Stadthaus*, the State House."

Paul gulped. His father had told him that the Stadthaus was the central headquarters of the Gestapo.

"They say a lot of people go into that building, but few come out," Luka said angrily. "They took me into the basement and into an interrogation room, almost like a cell. Three Gestapo men took turns interrogating me. They demanded to know if I was an Edelweiss Pirate and ordered me to give them names of other Pirates. They shoved one of our pamphlets under my nose and said it was useless to deny anything.

"But I refused to say a word." He looked around the group. "You know I'd never reveal a thing about any one of you." Murmurs floated across the campsite as Luka continued.

"When I refused to answer them, they slapped me around and warned me it was just the beginning, and things were going to get worse if I didn't talk."

The whole time Luka was recounting his story, Kiki sat staring straight ahead, unmoving. Paul couldn't tell what she was feeling. Anger that her brother had been arrested and interrogated? Relief that he had been released? Despair that things had come to this stage? Worry about what was to come next?

"If you can believe it, the worst part wasn't the beating," Luka continued. "The worst part was no sleep and no food. You become weak and confused. You lose control. I worried I might admit to something without realizing what I'd done." Luka's voice shook as he spoke. He paused and breathed in and out.

"But I told them nothing. And they couldn't pin anything on me. So finally, they said they were going to let me go. Before releasing me, they walked me through a courtyard where I saw three gallows standing side by side. One of the Gestapo officers pointed at them, and then he said, 'That's where you'll end up if we catch you again.'"

Paul felt the blood drain from his face. There was an eerie silence in the forest as if the birds and small animals had paused to listen to Luka. After a moment, he chuckled and smiled.

"Don't worry, my friends. My neck isn't in a noose yet, and I intend to keep it that way!"

The group let out their collective breath and started chattering. One after another, the Pirates lined up in front of Luka to shake his hand, slap him on the back, and tell him how glad they were to have him back. After his turn at congratulating Luka, Paul approached Kiki who was still quiet and standing apart from the group.

"Are you okay?" he asked.

"I was afraid I'd lost him, just like my father…." Her voice shook as it trailed off.

"Your brother is one of the bravest and strongest people I know," Paul said. And he meant it. But deep

in his heart, he knew that in times like these, bravery
and strength might not be enough.

CHAPTER 15
Thursday, October 27, 1938

The Pirates were still not ready to resume their resistance activities. Luka said it was better to stay quiet for a while longer. Kiki would signal Paul when it was time to get back to work. For the time being, Paul's evenings were now free, and he spent them at home with his parents who were delighted to have him around. "It's so nice to have you at home. You're out so much these days," Mama said, one night.

Paul usually diverted her curiosity by saying he was visiting Harold. "Harold's been upset ever since he burned his leg in that fire," Paul said. "I just want to keep him company and get his mind off of those things."

"You're a good friend," she replied.

Paul and his parents were gathered around the radio

after dinner. The Nazi-controlled radio station spewed out the usual broadcast about national pride, patriotism, and respect for Hitler. Papa tried to find a station from London, England that would broadcast some "real news," as he called it. Everyone knew that it was a treasonable offense to listen to overseas broadcasts, and anyone caught tuning in to something other than Nazi news would be jailed. But Papa didn't worry too much about that. "I need to know what's really happening in the world," he said as he turned the circular dial and listened to the shifting signals. "We're here in our own home. Who's going to hear us? No one's going to know."

Just as those words left Papa's lips, there was a sudden loud knock at the door. Paul jumped and stared at his father who quickly switched off the radio. Then, he placed a finger across his lips. Silence fell on the room. Paul swallowed uneasily. It was impossible that anyone could have heard the radio or their conversation. So that couldn't be the reason for the knock.

"Who could that be?" Mama whispered. "At this hour."

A moment passed and then the knocking resumed, louder and more insistent.

"Let me answer," Papa said, rising. "You stay here."

Paul trailed after his father to the front door and stood behind him while Papa took a deep breath, straightened the vest that he was wearing, and opened the door. Two men stood on the other side, each wearing a long gray overcoat and cap, with tall black boots. A band with a swastika encircled each of their arms.

One man clicked his heels together. "Gestapo!" he announced.

Paul sucked in his breath. The secret police of the Nazi government! The men who had taken Luka and interrogated and beaten him.

"Herr Ritter?" the man asked Papa.

"Yes?"

"We'd like to come in. We have a few questions we'd like to ask."

Paul could see Papa's hands shaking as he pulled the door open and stepped aside to allow the Gestapo to enter. Meanwhile, Paul's mind was racing. *Questions? Was this about the pamphlet drop? Had someone seen him and reported it? There was only person who could have done that. Ernst!*

Mama rose when the officers entered the sitting room. Her hand went to her throat and her eyes skipped from the officers to Papa to Paul and back to the Gestapo.

"Frau Ritter," the same man said, clicking his heels together again. The officer had a long, tapered face, and a narrow jaw that was pointed at the chin. His partner had said nothing so far. The smell of stale tobacco reached Paul from across the room. This man's eyes were placed just a bit too wide for his face. Those eyes roamed the room, moving from the paintings on the wall to the photographs on the table to the radio standing in the corner, finally coming to rest on Paul. Paul began to squirm under the stare.

"Please, sit down," Papa was saying.

"Thank you," the first man replied. "We'd prefer to stand. We don't think this will take long."

Sweat was gathering under Paul's arms and across his upper lip. He knew he needed to stay calm. He had to look composed. Paul willed his breathing to slow down, dropped his shoulders, and looked back at the Gestapo officer, meeting his stare.

"Would you please tell us what this is about?" Papa asked.

"Perhaps your son would like to tell us," the Gestapo replied.

Paul swallowed hard, trying not to gag or drop his eyes.

"Paul?" Mama asked. Her face was pinched and strained. "What are these men talking about?"

"I have no idea," Paul replied, finding his voice. Did he sound even enough?

"Perhaps you could give us some more information about what you want with our son," Papa said, moving over to stand next to Paul. He placed a hand on Paul's shoulder for protection and reassurance.

The Gestapo reached into his coat pocket and pulled

out a pamphlet. "We've had a report that your son may have been involved in some subversive activities at the train station. These were distributed by some young people we consider to be enemies of the Führer." He held the pamphlet out to Papa.

Paul barely heard what the officer was saying. His eyes were trained on the pamphlet that the man was holding out to his father, one of the pamphlets he had left at the train station the other night.

Papa extended a trembling hand to take the pamphlet. Then he reached into his pocket for his glasses, put them on, and began to read. His face was even paler than before when he passed the paper to Mama. She read it and gasped out loud.

"This is from a group," the Gestapo officer continued. "They call themselves the Edelweiss Pirates." He wrinkled his nose and sneered as he said the name. "They think they are being heroic with what they are calling acts of resistance around the country. But make no mistake, they are traitors. We must root them out and punish them. And that's what we intend to do."

"This is ridiculous," Mama cried, turning to Paul. "Our son would never participate in anything like that."

Thank goodness Paul had not said a word about his activities with the Pirates to his parents. They would never have been able to lie so convincingly for him. Their bewilderment now was genuine.

The same officer turned to Paul. "Perhaps you'd like to answer for yourself." He removed a small notebook from his pocket and flipped through it, finding a page that Paul could see was filling with writing. "The incident we are referring to took place on…on the evening of Wednesday, October nineteenth," he said, scanning through his notes. Then he looked up. "Where were you that night?"

Think! Think! Think! Paul's mind raced. What could he say that wouldn't get him or others into trouble? His mind was blank; his desperation was growing.

"Wednesday, the nineteenth?" Mama asked. "Why, that was one of the nights when you were at Harold's. Isn't that right, Paul?"

"Harold?" The Gestapo instantly picked up on the name while Paul's stomach plunged.

"Yes," Papa jumped in. "His friend, Harold Becker. He lives just around the corner. A red house. Both of the boys are members of the Hitler Youth—loyal and devoted members," he added. "Our son and Harold often get together in the evenings. I believe Paul was there that night." He turned to Paul. "Isn't that right?"

Paul gulped and nodded. He had no choice.

Meanwhile, the Gestapo officer was writing in his notebook. When he finished, he closed it up and replaced it in his pocket. "Good. We will certainly check your story with the other young man."

120

Paul couldn't even begin to think about how he would handle this nightmare with Harold. For now, all he thought was that the Gestapo were finished with him and were going to leave. He was wrong.

"Just one more thing," the officer said. "You won't mind if we look in your room."

His room! Paul's mind raced once more. Just before he had run off with Kiki that night at the train station, he had shoved a last pamphlet in his pocket, one that he hadn't dropped on the ground when Ernst called out to him. He had meant to get rid of the paper. But instead, when he got home, he had shoved the pamphlet in his top desk drawer along with his Edelweiss pin. He didn't know why he had kept the paper. He was still planning to get rid of it, especially after Luka's arrest, but that just never happened. How stupid of him to have left it there.

There was no time to think about what to do. The Gestapo officer was walking toward his bedroom.

CHAPTER 16

If Paul was scared before, that was nothing compared with what he was feeling now. His heart was banging in his chest as if it were looking for a way to get out. Adrenaline flooded through every part of his body. One thought pounded in his brain: His Edelweiss pin and the discarded pamphlet were in the top drawer of his desk, just waiting to be found. This was the evidence the Gestapo needed to tie him to the pamphlet drop. Paul had to think of a way out of this and fast.

He strode alongside the Gestapo officer and dashed inside of his room just ahead of him. But there was no time to do anything. The officer was right on his heels and was inside the door before Paul could even turn around. Paul's eyes skimmed across the items in his room: his bed, chest of drawers, bookshelf, and of course, the desk. *Where to stand?* he wondered. If he chose to stand next to the desk, would that be too obvious? On the other hand, standing far from it might make it seem like he was trying to pull attention away from it.

"You seem to be nervous," the officer was saying. "Is something wrong?"

Paul was chewing on a fingernail, but quickly dropped his hand by his side, rubbing his sweaty palm against his trousers. He shook his head. "No, sir, of course not," he finally replied. "I just don't like anyone rummaging through my personal things."

The officer stared long and hard at Paul. "This won't take long." With that, he walked to Paul's dresser and opened the first drawer, digging through his clothing. First drawer done, he closed it and moved on to the second one, and then the third. It felt to Paul as if time was standing still, or moving slower than mud. How much longer would this man be here? And how thoroughly was he going to search?

The Gestapo officer had finished with the dresser and moved to the bookshelf. He began to remove several books, tossing them onto Paul's bed, and then reaching his hand behind the books to investigate the back of each shelf. For Paul, the search was becoming more unbearable by the second. His eyes darted once more to his desk and to the top drawer, desperate to find a way out of this disaster.

The Gestapo officer started to go through the second shelf. He removed several more books, searched again behind the volumes, and then bent to look at the third shelf. All the while he did not say a word. He methodically and carefully rifled through shelf after shelf, moving his hands between and behind every book. Finally, he stood and looked around. For a brief moment, Paul dared to believe that the search was over. Perhaps the officer would be satisfied going through his dresser and bookshelf and would leave. But that was not the case. With his heart sinking faster than a lead weight, Paul watched the officer finally walk over to his desk. First, he surveyed the papers that sat on top: a couple of school notebooks, pens, and a mathematics text. He lifted the notebooks, moved the textbook aside, and flipped through the papers. Finally, his hand moved to the handle of the top drawer. Paul's mouth was as dry as sand. He closed his eyes as he heard the drawer creak open an inch.

"What do we have here?"

It was all over. In another second, the pamphlet and pin would be found, and Paul would be arrested and taken away. Who knew what punishment he would be made to suffer? He squeezed his eyes tightly together and held his breath.

"I see you have something wonderful that you're keeping in your desk!"

What? Paul opened his eyes a crack and saw that the officer had pulled a book out of his top drawer. He straightened and turned around, smiling for the first time since his arrival.

The book he pulled out was called *The Poisonous Serpent.* It was written by the same man who had written *The Poisonous Mushroom*, the book that Herr Bentz had used in class, that terrible story that compared Jews to lethal mushrooms. Paul would never have had such a book in his collection. But Ernst had leant it to him, bragging about this next installment, and urging Paul to read it. Paul hadn't wanted to arouse any suspicion, so he had taken the book, shoved it into his drawer, and forgotten about it. Now, he smiled weakly back at the Gestapo officer.

"Yes, we've been reading this and other books like it in school."

The officer flipped through the pages, stopped at one, and read one line aloud.

"The Jews do to people what poisonous snakes do to people."

He nodded approvingly. "So true! But I don't know why you're keeping it hidden in your desk. You must put it in a place where it can be seen." With that, he carried the book over to Paul's bookshelf and placed it on a top shelf. Then he stood back to look at it. "Much better!"

For a moment, Paul thought he might be off the hook. He dared to hope that the officer might now leave. He even had the crazy thought that he'd have Ernst to thank for loaning him that terrible book. But when Paul glanced back at the desk, he could just make out a corner of the pamphlet sitting inside his open desk drawer. And beside it was his Edelweiss pin. If the officer searched any further, he would find those things immediately. And sure enough, Paul watched as the officer walked back to the desk and bent to open the drawer further.

Just then, there was a knock at Paul's bedroom door. The second officer, the one with the wide eyes who reeked of tobacco, poked his head inside.

"Sir," the second officer said, clicking his heels together and bowing slightly. "We have to report back to Gestapo headquarters before eight o'clock."

The first officer turned slightly to face his partner, though his hand was still on the handle of the desk drawer. And the pamphlet was still there looking to Paul like a beacon glowing in the dark, calling out to be seen. The officer hesitated a moment.

"It's getting late, sir," the tobacco-smelling man said.

Another hesitation, and then the first officer shut the drawer with a soft thud. "Yes, you're right." He stood up straight, adjusting his coat. "I think I've seen enough here. There's nothing to find." Then he turned to Paul. "That's all for now."

With that, he clicked his heels together one last time, and extended his arm in a salute to Hitler. Weakly, Paul did the same. Then, the officer moved to the door and walked out.

Paul sank onto his bed feeling as if his legs were about to buckle. A moment later, Papa entered his room followed by Mama. Their eyes were round with worry.

"Paul, we need to talk about what just happened—" Papa began.

"Not now, Papa. Please!" Paul knew he owed his parents some kind of explanation. But all he wanted to do was crawl into bed and try to forget everything that had just happened.

Papa looked puzzled. "Paul," he said again. "Do you have any idea why the Gestapo were here? Why did they come looking for you?"

Paul took a deep and shaky breath. "No, Papa, no idea." A lingering smell of tobacco still hung in the air.

"You're not keeping anything from us, are you?" his mother asked. She still looked as if she'd seen a ghost.

Paul's jaw tightened. "No Mama, no Papa. Of course, I'm not hiding anything. You don't need to worry."

Papa looked as if he wanted to say more. But instead, he took Mama by the arm and left Paul's room. Paul closed his eyes. Relief surged through him. His pamphlet and pin had not been discovered. He was safe. And then, he was struck with a horrifying thought.

Harold!

CHAPTER 17

Friday, October 28, 1938

Another sleepless night. Paul had suffered too many of them lately. But this time, he knew he had to get to Harold's house first thing in the morning. What would Harold say if the Gestapo came to his door to ask him about Paul? If the Gestapo had already gone to Harold's house last night, Paul felt he was already doomed. If they hadn't yet visited Harold, then could he convince his best friend to lie for him?

Mama was already in the kitchen when Paul walked in. "You're up early today," she said, lifting her eyes from the tea she was drinking. There were dark circles ringing Mama's eyes and deep lines creasing her forehead.

"Didn't sleep much," Paul mumbled.

"Was it the visit from the Gestapo?"

"Yes."

Mama sighed. "It kept me up, too." She stared at her son. "I'm worried about you, Paul. You'd tell us if you were in trouble, wouldn't you?" The circles under Mama's eyes seemed to darken as she asked the question.

Paul didn't answer.

"I know we've always told you to follow your heart and remember who you are in the midst of this madness that's overtaken our country. But we never want you to put yourself in any danger."

And I don't want to put you and Papa in danger, Paul thought to himself.

Mama's voice caught as she breathed out. Tears gathered in the corners of her eyes. She stood and walked toward Paul, reaching her arms up to hug him. "Please be safe," she whispered in his ear.

✦ ✦ ✦

Paul dashed out the door and ran over to Harold's house only to discover that his friend had left early for school.

"He said he had an assignment that he had to turn in before classes today," Harold's mother explained when she opened the door. "You may be able to catch up."

Paul shouted his thanks over his shoulder and bolted down the street, running all the way to school. Up ahead, he could see the other students standing in the schoolyard. His eyes searched frantically for Harold, but Paul couldn't see him. There were too many students crowding around, practically on top of each other. Paul pushed his way into a cluster of students, and when Harold wasn't there, he waded into a second cluster, and then a third. Each passing second only made his apprehension swell. The bell was going to ring any minute. Just when he thought he was too late, he spotted Harold standing in a far corner of the yard, all alone.

Paul walked quickly over to his friend. He didn't want to draw attention to himself, and he certainly didn't want to run into Ernst. He finally reached Harold and leaned up against the wall next to him. The two were silent, not even greeting one another. Paul didn't know how to begin, or what to say. And then, Harold started to talk.

"They came to my house last night—the Gestapo. They wanted to know if you had come over to my place on Wednesday, the nineteenth. They had the date written down, along with my name. They talked about the vandalism in the city."

Paul's stomach lurched and he squeezed his eyes shut. "What did you say to them?" he croaked out.

Harold turned to look at him. "I told them you were at my house that night."

Paul spun around. "You said that?"

"Yes." Harold leaned his head back against the wall.

"Look, I don't know what you're up to. And I'm not sure I want to know. But you're my friend. That's what's most important."

Once again, Paul didn't know what to say. He squeezed his eyes shut once more as a feeling of complete relief flowed through his body.

"You're just lucky my parents weren't home last night," Harold continued. "I wouldn't have been able to lie if they had been in the room with me."

Paul exhaled in one long slow breath. "Harold, I'm so…so grateful. You have no idea." Paul stared out at the schoolyard. Ernst was across the way, surrounded by a group of students. His arms were moving in circles; his chest was puffed out. He seemed to be telling some kind of story. The students around him were laughing as he held court.

Harold let his head fall back against the wall, and he stared up at the sky, dotted with clouds. "Whatever you're…doing…is it something good?" he finally asked.

"It is! Trust me on this, Harold. It's for the good of all of us," Paul replied.

Harold let out a big sigh. "I'm not as brave as you are," he said. "I never will be."

Paul turned to face his friend. "Harold, you just lied to the Gestapo to protect me. I'd say that makes you pretty courageous."

CHAPTER 18

Sunday, November 6, 1938

The Pirates gathered under the iron bridge to prepare for another act of sabotage. There had been no activity in over a week. When Paul let Kiki know about the visit from the Gestapo, she had reported it to Luka who decided that it was better for the Pirates to disappear for a while. Paul and Harold had not said much more to each other about the interrogation from the Gestapo. At the last Hitler Youth meeting, Ernst had watched both of them searchingly. Paul returned the stare, looking him squarely in the eye. Harold, on the other hand, seemed to shrink into himself under Ernst's scrutiny. Paul wasn't about to yield to Ernst or let him know that he was afraid. But the truth was, there were butterflies the size of soccer balls bouncing around in his stomach.

He still didn't know for certain that Ernst was the one who had gone to the Gestapo about him and the pamphlets. But who else could have done it? And was it only a matter of time before he or one of the other Pirates was caught?

Under the bridge, he shook the thought away and looked around for Kiki, finding her stuffing something into her backpack. She had passed him in the school hallway before the weekend, flashing her Edelweiss pin as a sign that the group was going to meet.

"So, what's the plan tonight?" Paul asked.

"A special operation," she replied, eyes lighting up. "It's so easy for the Gestapo to get around the city. So, we thought we'd put a halt to that—at least for a while."

Paul frowned. *What did that mean?*

Kiki smiled. "You'll see." And that was all she was prepared to say.

A short while later the group set out, moving into the main part of the city. They walked in a pack led by Luka, keeping their heads down, their eyes attentive, and their minds alert. Any noise drove them into the shadows. They were careful to stay away from streetlamps and from cars that drove past. Most of the time, they hugged the walls of buildings, skirted around monuments, and paused behind tree trunks. It was raining, a steady, cold downpour that quickly soaked through Paul's jacket. He shivered and pulled his cap further down over his face, watching as drops of water dribbled from the rim and joined the puddles that were growing below his feet.

Paul was not sure where they were going. The Pirates never liked to reveal too much of their plans in advance of a raid. Luka knew, he had organized everything. And Kiki always seemed to know. She acted like his right-hand person, relaying information, organizing the details, and taking care of the specifics of each operation. But the others were usually kept in the dark. That way, if someone was caught, they could legitimately say they had no clue what was going on. Paul knew that the plans would be revealed in due time. He followed the person in front of him like a school child being led into a classroom. He trusted Luka, Kiki, and everyone else in the group.

The Pirates kept walking, weaving in between buildings and down small streets and alleyways. They moved this way and that, until they finally emerged in a large square where Luka signaled them to stop. Paul knew where they were. It was the Altstadt—the Old Town, a central area of Düsseldorf filled with cobblestone streets that created a maze of lanes and pathways, like the veins of a spider web. Up ahead was a building that Paul knew well—everyone in Düsseldorf did. It was the Stadthaus—the State House, the building that had been turned into the central headquarters for the Gestapo. This was where Luka had been brought the night of his arrest. Paul shuddered and looked around, listening to his own quick breathing competing with the sound of the steady rain. Surely, the Pirates were not going to raid this building! That would be too dangerous.

Instead of heading forward, Luka led everyone around it to a big lot at the back of the building, filled with cars—black, sleek, shining even in the darkness, and glistening in the rainfall. A swastika flag hung, limp and heavy with rain, from the front of every hood. These were the cars that were used by the Gestapo, parked here in this unsupervised lot.

The group surrounded Luka in a tight circle.

"Here's the plan," he said, keeping his voice low. He opened his backpack and pulled out a bag like the one that Paul had seen Kiki stuff into her backpack. It held what looked like gray granulated powder. "It's sand," Luka whispered. "Line up in front of me or Kiki and you'll each get a bag. Then pick a car, open the hood, unscrew the oil tank cap, and pour it in."

Paul frowned. He wasn't sure what that would do.

As if reading his mind, Luka continued. "Sand will clog up the whole engine in these cars." He smiled. "This fleet won't be going anywhere once we're done with it."

This was a crazy plan to be sure, Paul thought as he lined up for his bag of sand. But it was ingenious, a perfect way to stop the Gestapo from traveling around the city—at least for some time. But also, it was a perfect way to infuriate them. How long would it take them to repair the damage?

Paul grabbed a bag and headed for a car, quietly lifting the hood and peering under it. He didn't know much about cars—he wasn't really that interested in how they worked. He'd helped his father fill their car with gas many times. But beyond that, he rarely looked under the hood. Where was the oil cap, anyway? *Ah, no problem*, he realized. It was clearly marked. He turned the cap to the left, removed it, and began to pour the sand in from the bag he'd been given.

Kiki was working on a car next to him. She was focused, her brow furrowed, and she chewed on her bottom lip as she poured sand into the tank. She looked up at Paul, smiled briefly, and gave him a quick thumbs-up as she finished with one car, carefully and quietly lowered the hood, and moved on to another. It didn't take long for the group to work through the twenty or more automobiles. All the while, Luka and some of the others stood guard, ready to signal the group if there was any trouble. Finally, Luka gave a low whistle. They needed to finish quickly and get out of there before a Gestapo official or someone else saw what they were doing.

Paul finished up with his last car, closed the hood, and joined Kiki and the others. They headed down another laneway as a group, coming to a stop at the corner. Just before they all dispersed, Luka pulled them together in one last tight circle.

"We'll lay low again for a while," he said. "Watch for your signals and you'll know when it's time for another operation."

Paul met Kiki's eyes and nodded. She smiled back at him.

"This one is going to drive the Gestapo crazy," Luka added, grinning in the dark. "Great job, everyone!"

Someone clapped Paul on the back. All around him, the Pirates were shaking hands and whispering, *well done*. The rain that had been falling all evening had become stronger, cascading in gushing streams. Paul was soaked to the skin, but he didn't care. His face glowed from the work he had just finished, and he felt more exhilarated than he'd felt in a long time. The same feeling as running a race. The thrill of crossing a finish line. Kiki was right, he thought as he said good-bye to his comrades and headed back home. By day, he had to be silent, going through the paces of pretending to go along with the enemy—pretending to be one of them. But by night, he was a rebel, standing up for what he believed was right and decent. And for now, that was enough.

CHAPTER 19

Monday, November 7, 1938

Franz was in a rage. News of the sabotage of the Nazi fleet had spread throughout the city. Everyone in the Hitler Youth knew about it. No one, Paul least of all, was surprised by Franz's reaction. He spent practically the entire next meeting ranting about what had been done to the Gestapo cars and what would happen when the culprits were caught.

"The punishment for this act will be brutal," he shouted into his megaphone. "We will hunt down the criminals who did this. No stone will be left unturned."

He had said almost the same thing when the Pirates had graffitied the walls of the city. He had sworn that the "criminals" would be caught for that act, too. But no one had been arrested. And Paul knew that there was no evidence for the Gestapo to follow this time. He believed that the Pirates had been thorough and careful. They had covered their tracks well. No one would be found. That didn't, however, stop the Gestapo from going house to house to see if anyone had seen or heard anything. Paul got that information from Ernst.

"They're bringing people in for questioning," Ernst said when the meeting finally ended and Franz had dismissed the group. Paul always tried to dodge Ernst at the end of a meeting. He and Harold walked away as quickly as they could to avoid him. But there was no getting away from him today. He caught up with them and insisted that they walk home together, pushing their bikes.

"They'll catch whoever did this," Ernst said.

"Have they found anything?" Paul asked, keeping his voice as casual as he could.

Ernst shook his head. "Not yet. But they will!" His eyes flashed. "It was probably the Jews. We'll round up a bunch of them and send them to the concentration camps."

Paul glanced at Ernst, for the first time feeling deeply troubled by the whole mission. Not only were the Nazis angry at what had been done to their fleet of cars, they were ashamed that someone or some group had embarrassed them like this—and all under their very noses! Humiliation was not something that the Nazis took lightly. Paul knew that they didn't need an excuse to go after Jewish people. And he didn't want Jews to pay the price for something that he and the Pirates had done. After all, he had joined the Pirates not only as an act of resistance against Hitler, but also because he was motivated by his deep concern for Analia, her family, and all Jewish citizens. Paul feared that the Nazis' payback would be brutal and the Jews were an easy target. Would Analia and her family be caught up in some kind of horrible punishment for something they had nothing to do with?

Ernst caught Harold looking at him. "What are you staring at?"

"No…nothing," Harold stammered.

"Do you know something? Are you hiding something?"

Harold swallowed hard. His eyes darted over to Paul who squirmed and then shot a glance back at Ernst. Ernst's jaw was clenched, and he looked like a tightly wound spring about to snap. He wanted someone to lash out at. And it looked as if Harold was about to become his target.

"No…no…I don't…I know…I don't know…." Harold was becoming more flustered. He knew nothing about the Nazi cars. But Ernst wasn't buying it.

He stopped and glared at Harold. Then, without warning, he exploded. He threw his bike down onto the ground, grabbed Harold's arm, and wrenched it hard behind his back. Harold's bike went flying. His face twisted and he cried out in pain.

"What are you hiding, Becker?" Ernst demanded. "What do you know?" He pulled Harold's arm further up his back.

"Nothing!" Harold yelped. "I don't know anything."

"Stop it! You're hurting him!" Paul yelled, abandoning his own bike and jumping in to help his friend. He pulled and yanked and tried to pry Ernst's hands away from Harold's arm, but Ernst held firm.

"Back off, Ritter," Ernst said as he pulled on Harold's arm again.

Paul threw himself up against Ernst with all his might, and with one final yell, he managed to break the hold he had on Harold. "I said stop it!"

Ernst released Harold, pushed him to the ground, and stepped back. He was breathing hard. A line of spit had dribbled onto his chin. He reached up and wiped it away. Ernst looked at Paul, eyes narrowing. "If you're in on something, I'll find out." Then he glared at Harold. "You're too much of a weakling to get involved."

With that, he retrieved his bicycle from the ground, threw his leg over the seat, and rode away at a furious pace. Paul helped Harold off the ground. "Are you okay?"

Harold was shaking and breathing hard. He rubbed

his shoulder and moved his arm in a slow circle. But he shook Paul's hand off and stepped away from him. "Ernst won't let up, you know. None of them will. If you're involved in any of this, you have to stop."

Paul didn't reply. He retrieved Harold's bike and tried to clean the dirt off, but Harold pushed his arm away once more.

"Leave me alone," he said. "Just leave me alone." With that, Harold jumped on his bike and rode away, leaving Paul standing on the road.

Paul stared after his friend and then went to get his own bike, pushing off for home. His head was a jumble of thoughts. He had to find a way to reassure Harold; tell him that they'd be sure to avoid Ernst in the future, and that Paul would be there to look out for his friend. But he knew in his heart that wouldn't be enough. He knew Harold was afraid. And what's more, Paul was afraid, too.

CHAPTER 20
Tuesday, November 8, 1938

When Paul appeared at Harold's door early the next morning, his mother said he had already left for school again.

"Is there something going on between the two of you?" Frau Becker asked when Paul knocked on the door. "I'd hate to think you've had a fight or something. You're such good friends."

"Everything's okay, Frau Becker," Paul said, swallowing hard. It was another lie. "I guess I just forgot that Harold was going early today. I'll catch him at school."

Paul said good-bye and broke into an easy jog, trying to rehearse in his mind what he would say to Harold when he got to him. *Please, don't be mad at me. Everything is going to be okay. If anything goes wrong, I'll look out for you.* But everything sounded so idiotic and childish in light of the threats from Ernst and Franz and the Gestapo. He'd have to figure this out once he saw Harold. He truly believed in his heart that his friend would not stay angry with him. The truth was, they needed each other. They were friends, and friends had to stick together—in good times, and especially in hard times.

In the end, he had no opportunity to say anything to Harold. When Paul arrived at school, the students were already being walked into the building and told to assemble in the auditorium. There was an important announcement that everyone needed to hear, and Herr Bentz was the one who was going to deliver it.

"Attention! Attention!" he called, standing in front of a microphone and facing the students who stopped shuffling and whispering and began to come to order. Paul could see Harold standing to one side. He tried to get his friend's attention, but Harold would not look his way no matter how much Paul willed him to. Herr Bentz waited for complete silence. Only when it was dead quiet in the room did he begin to talk. And what he said made Paul's blood run cold.

Herr Bentz said that a high-level Nazi diplomat by the name of Ernst vom Rath had been shot by none other than a seventeen-year-old Jewish teen named Herschel Grynszpan. This young Jewish man had gone to the embassy in Paris where vom Rath was posted and had shot him five times in the stomach.

"Our Führer sent his personal physician to treat vom Rath," Herr Bentz said, his voice eerily calm. "But despite the efforts of several doctors, vom Rath succumbed to his wounds. He is dead."

Murmurs floated through the auditorium.

"Dead at the hands of a cowardly Jew!"

More murmurs, this time mixed with hostile mumbles and fists pumped into the air.

Paul thought his head might explode. He was already sick with worry that the Nazis were going to target Jews following the vandalism of the Gestapo fleet of cars. But Paul knew that this event would take the Nazis over the edge. They would be out for blood, and Jews were going to suffer.

The rest of the day passed in a blur for Paul. In class, Herr Bentz continued to rant about the murder of vom Rath. He hinted that the Nazis would do something to retaliate. "Something bigger than anything that has been seen so far," he said.

What could that possibly mean? Vague threats like that were almost worse than knowing exactly what was going to happen. This warning just hung in the air like low clouds signaling the approach of a menacing storm. Paul abandoned any thought of talking to Harold. He had to find Kiki and see what the Pirates thought about all of this. And sure enough, when he passed her in the hallway later that day, she flashed her Edelweiss pin and quickly moved on.

Paul headed for the campsite as soon as class was dismissed. He was surprised to see several new faces in the group; a man and a woman, and next to them, a young girl. The man had a dark cap that covered most of his red hair, and the woman had a green scarf wrapped tightly around her head. They each had a yellow star sewn on to their jackets. But it was the little girl who captured Paul's attention. One hand grasped her mother's coat; the thumb of her other hand was planted firmly in her mouth. Her hair was as red as her father's, and her nose was so freckled that the spots nearly blended into one another. She also had a star sewn onto her coat. Paul gulped as thoughts of Analia charged through his mind. This was a Jewish family! What were they doing here?

"Their store was ransacked by the Nazis today—a store I used to go to for sweets," Kiki said coming to stand next to Paul. "Herr Blidner," she pointed at the man who stood clutching his wife and daughter, "and his wife ran it for as long as I can remember. Frau Blidner used to pass out candies to all the kids who went by. Today, the Nazis walked into their store with clubs and started destroying everything. Before they left, they said they'd be back and then things would get even worse.

I was on my way here to the campsite when I saw it happen. I waited until the Nazis had left, and then told the family to come with me. I couldn't leave them there knowing those thugs were going to come back. We're going to try to help them."

Paul glanced over at the little girl; she couldn't have been more than three or four, but her eyes seemed old, as if she had already witnessed too much trouble in her young life. "What can we do?" he asked.

"They'll stay here until we can find a safe place for them to hide and people who agree to hide them." She looked at Paul. "Not everyone is out to get the Jews. We know some people who are willing to help."

The rest of the pirates were huddled in a circle around a small fire. Their heads were bent together, their faces gloomy.

"We know something is in the works," Luka said after Paul had greeted everyone and joined the group. In the few weeks since Luka's arrest, the bruises and cuts on his face had faded to almost nothing. But while his scars had nearly disappeared, his resolve to get back at the Nazis had only deepened. "I'm afraid that attacks like the one against the Blidner family are only the beginning. But we can't seem to get much information about what's going to happen."

That wasn't good. It meant that the Nazis had closed ranks and were keeping whatever this retaliation was a complete secret. Usually, they bragged about things they were planning. Not this time.

"Whatever this is, it's so much bigger than only getting back at the Jews here in Düsseldorf," Luka continued.

Paul remembered what Herr Bentz had said: "Something bigger than anything that has been seen so far." He relayed it to the group.

"I'm afraid that Jews across Germany and possibly in other countries are in danger," Luka said.

Kiki had been unusually quiet. Paul moved around the circle until he was next to her. "What do you think they're going to do?" he asked.

Kiki shook her head. "I don't know. The Jewish teenager who killed vom Rath—he went to look for vom Rath after his own parents were arrested and deported to the concentration camps. It doesn't excuse what he did; murder is a crime no matter what. But, can you imagine how desperate he must have felt?"

Desperation was like fear, Paul thought. Sometimes it made you close down. But sometimes it drove you to act. In this case, so many were going to pay for a Jewish boy's desperation.

"You know, vom Rath was a native of Düsseldorf."

Paul stared at Kiki. He hadn't known that.

"It's as if one of their own has died."

It was probably another reason why the Nazis were so enraged. First, there was the sabotage of their fleet of cars by his group. And then the murder of a high-ranking German official and "son" of Düsseldorf, not just some random citizen. Paul shuddered as another moment of regret over the Pirates' activities passed over him. Perhaps they had stirred the anger of the Nazis too much. Perhaps they were part of the desperation that so many were feeling. But how could the Pirates have known that this assassination was going to take place? And just days after their own actions?

Paul left the circle to go over to the Jewish family. They had not moved, but Paul could tell from their faces that they were taking in every word of the conversation that the Pirates were having. He smiled at the couple and then bent down to the little girl.

"Hello," he said.

She stared at Paul, thumb still lodged in her mouth.

"I'm Paul. Can you tell me your name?"

"Her name is Stella," Frau Blidner jumped in, extending her arm like a bird's wing to wrap around her daughter.

"Hello, Stella. Can you tell me how old you are?"

A slight hesitation, and then she raised four fingers to the sky.

Paul nodded, eyes widening. "Four is a very important age." He turned away from Stella, eyes searching the ground. When he turned back to her, he was holding something in his hand. "Do you see this rock, Stella?"

It lay on Paul's palm, gray and smooth with yellow spots across both sides, just like the freckles on Stella's nose. "If you ever feel afraid, just hold on to it, and rub it, and it will help you feel less scared."

Stella's eyes narrowed with doubt.

"You're probably wondering how that happens, right?"

She nodded.

"Well, I'm really not sure myself. But I have a rock just like this one. And when I hold it, I feel better." He held the rock out to her. "It's worth a try, isn't it? We could all use something to hold onto when we're afraid."

Stella hesitated a minute. She removed her thumb from her mouth and reached a tentative hand out to take the rock. She stared down at it, and then placed it in her coat pocket. A moment later, her thumb found its way back into her mouth. Stella's parents smiled gratefully at Paul as he rose and turned back to his group.

Luka was still talking. "Be strong, everyone. We can't let this news break us down."

"What are we going to do?" Paul asked Kiki.

She clenched a fist against her leg and pressed her lips together. "Until we know more, we just have to keep our eyes open."

CHAPTER 21

Wednesday, November 9, 1938, 5:00 p.m.

It didn't take long for the Nazi plans to reveal themselves. A Hitler Youth meeting was scheduled for the very next day—a hasty announcement that Herr Bentz made at school.

"All members of the Hitler Youth are ordered to gather at the fairground after class today. The League of German Girls are also ordered to show up to their meetings. Go home, change into your uniforms, and report for duty." Herr Bentz's face was as grim as it had been the day before.

Paul glanced over at Harold who returned his stare, a troubled look in his eyes. Harold slunk down into his seat and lowered his head. By contrast, most of the other students in the class seemed revved up by the announcement. They were grinning and jabbing one another in the arm.

"I told you something was going to happen," Ernst said, leaning over to whisper gleefully to Paul. "And it's going to be big. I just know it."

By the time Paul and Harold and the others had assembled at the fairground later that day, the air was charged with excitement. Franz was on the stage huddling with several unfamiliar, older-looking men. They looked important, Paul thought, maybe Franz's superiors, leaders in the Hitler Youth who were there to oversee whatever this event was going to be. The appearance of these official-looking people did not make Paul feel any better. While the men clustered onstage, the other boys stood around looking slightly confused. They were ready for action, and now they had to wait. A low murmur washed across the field. Paul shivered and wrapped his arms around his body. The jacket that the Hitler Youth had issued for the colder weather was heavy, and the shorts that all the boys wore in the summer had been replaced by long pants. But in this moment, the warm clothing did little to stop Paul from shaking.

"I don't like this one bit," Harold muttered beside Paul. Their argument from the day before was forgotten, replaced by the unspoken agreement that it was wiser to stick together. "It's so much better when they're ordering us around," Harold continued. "When they get quiet like this and put their heads together, it makes me even more nervous."

Paul had exactly the same thought.

The sun was already starting to go down on the horizon when Franz finally lifted his megaphone and ordered the boys to line up in rows. His face was sinister.

"You've all heard of the murder of our dear comrade, Ernst vom Rath."

Murmured assents rolled across the crowd of boys.

"Vom Rath was a loyal member of the Nazi party, and a great friend of our beloved Führer. His murder was committed by a cowardly Jew!"

More murmurs, just like at the assembly when Herr Bentz had delivered this news. And just like at the school assembly, boys in the crowd shouted out, "Down with the Jews!"

Franz raised his hand to silence everyone. He smiled. "Yes, the Jews are indeed a curse. And we won't let them get away with this. It's time to show the Jews of Düsseldorf and in all of Germany that they are insects that need to be stamped out!"

All of Germany! What could that possibly mean? wondered Paul.

"Our glorious Führer has decreed that it's time to teach the Jews of Europe a lesson. And all of you will have the honor of taking part."

Despite the frigid air, that comment prompted a

trickle of cold sweat to wind its way down Paul's back. What lesson? And how were they to be involved in it? Paul felt Harold on one side of him shudder. Ernst on his other side grinned from ear to ear. "I told you it's going to be big," he whispered.

Franz barked more orders into his megaphone for the boys to begin the march into town. "Keep your formation! Follow your comrade in front of you. Remember that you represent the Hitler Youth. You represent our glorious Führer himself."

"Yes, troop leader!" the boys shouted back as they began to march, lifting their knees higher and higher, and swinging their arms back and forth.

Paul moved with them, keeping his eyes glued to the back of the head of the boy in front of him. A feeling of dread was rising up in Paul's chest in anticipation of what was going to happen. Making Jews clean the streets of Düsseldorf had been bad enough. Without even knowing what was to come, Paul believed in his heart that this was going to be so much worse.

He could see and smell the smoke before he saw the fire. Thick clouds rose into the air and floated by him in a haze, accompanied by the bitter taste of something burning that filled his nose and the back of his throat. His eyes began to itch and stream. He reached up to rub them; his sight was blurred. Boys all around him were coughing and sputtering. The orderly lines that

Franz had insisted on were becoming jumbled as boys tripped over their own feet, trying to avoid the murky clouds of smoke.

"Stay in your formations!" Franz barked.

Paul squeezed his eyes shut to stop the stinging, and then pried them open, straining to look over the heads of the boys who marched in front of him. At first, all he could see were black mountains of smoke encasing a structure and mushrooming up into the sky. It had to be a burning building, Paul thought. But he didn't know which one. He glanced around. They were approaching Kasernenstrasse, the Jewish section of Düsseldorf. It was where Analia lived. And in that moment of recognition, Paul's heart plummeted. The building on fire up ahead was the New Synagogue of Düsseldorf, the only large building in this part of the city.

"Halt!" Franz shouted, as everyone rounded a corner.

And sure enough, there it was. The synagogue was lit up, flames shooting from its roof and windows. Several smaller shops on either side of the street were also on fire. Nazi soldiers and German police were everywhere. But they weren't there to control the fire. They were there to fuel it. Paul watched in horror as soldier after soldier heaved torches and flares toward the synagogue, tossing them inside the front door and onto the roof. Citizens of Düsseldorf stood shoulder to shoulder with the Nazis, throwing sticks and rocks at the building.

Other police stood by, watching the scene and doing nothing. A sudden plume of fire exploded upward into the blackness, illuminating the sky and accompanied by more clouds of soot and gas. It choked Paul, sucking the air out of his lungs. The smell, thick and noxious, filled Paul's lungs, choking him. He coughed and doubled over as if he'd been punched in the stomach. The boys shuffled and jostled one another trying to evade the smoke. It was like trying to dodge raindrops. It was everywhere and growing thicker by the minute.

Paul searched the crowd frantically, wondering if the Pirates were anywhere nearby. But even if they were there, what could they do? They were just a handful of young people and this mob was out of control. A group of girls was huddled across the way. From their uniforms, Paul knew they had to be with the League of German Girls. One of their troop leaders was shouting orders at them. Was Kiki in that group? Could she also see what was happening to the synagogue? Did she feel as helpless as Paul?

Franz came to stand next to the boys. "This is how we treat the Jews!" he shouted, trying to make his voice heard above the sound of the fire and the turmoil of people running in every direction. His face was contorted into a strange combination of rage and glee. "We will destroy their synagogues and burn them to the ground. And all of you will help make this happen."

How? Paul thought wildly.

"Find some rocks," Franz yelled. "The bigger and heavier the better. Throw them at the windows of that synagogue and listen to the shattering glass."

To demonstrate, Franz reached down and found a rock that was sharp and jagged. Then he turned toward the building and threw it into a window. Glass shards, fueled by the fire, exploded into the air and rained down on the sidewalk, already littered with glass, metal, and wood.

This was the cue that the boys had been waiting for. It was as if Franz had unleashed them from a pen. With whoops of joy that echoed into the night air, the boys scattered and fell to their knees, searching for rocks and stones and pieces of wood and metal, throwing them at the burning synagogue building with all their might, each throw accompanied by a shriek and a howl.

Paul couldn't move. His feet seemed glued to the ground as he watched in horror, the scene unfolding in front of him. Harold, standing next to him was just as stunned. His mouth was open, his eyes bulged, gasping for air as if he were being deprived of oxygen.

"I don't want to do this," Harold whispered.

"I'm not going to listen to them," Paul replied, as much to himself as to Harold. "I don't care what happens."

Franz marched over to the two of them and planted

himself directly in front of Harold, feet spread apart, hands on his hips.

"What is the matter with the two of you?" he demanded. "Didn't you hear my order? I said to find a rock and throw it."

He was shouting at both of them but he was staring at Harold, who withered under his glare. Harold fell to his knees and began to search the ground. He finally found a small stone, hardly more than a pebble. He stood and tossed it weakly toward the building. It didn't go very far and rolled feet away from the synagogue door.

Franz grabbed Harold by the collar and pulled him up to his face, practically nose to nose. Harold stiffened and closed his eyes, waiting to be bombarded with more commands and insults. But before Franz could shout more orders, there was another commotion up ahead. A group of people were being marched in front of the burning synagogue. Their heads were lowered, their feet stumbled across the debris. There must have been more than one hundred of them.

Paul knew immediately that they were Jews. The stars sewn onto their jackets were practically lit up in the fiery sky, as yellow as the flames from the synagogue that were still shooting skyward behind them. Several of the men wore skullcaps on their heads. They swayed back and forth as they walked, eyes closed as if in prayer. Women held on to their husbands and children. Elderly couples hugged each other.

"They're burning our beautiful synagogue," one old man shouted, his voice wailing into the night air.

"Somebody, help us!" another cried.

Nazi guards were everywhere, surrounding the Jews and prodding them forward. Several people stumbled and nearly fell as the guards jabbed them with their rifle butts and ordered them to keep moving.

Franz, momentarily distracted, released Harold and straightened his jacket. "Look this way, boys," he shouted again. "You are about to witness another great moment."

Paul couldn't hear a thing. Sounds were muffled in his ears. Franz continued to shout something, but Paul didn't know what. All he could do was stare ahead, mouth open, looking intently at the group of Jews slowly moving forward in front of him. And he could not take his eyes off one person in particular.

It was Analia.

CHAPTER 22

Wednesday, November 9, 1938, 6:00 p.m.

Nazi soldiers continued to encircle the group of Jewish people, corralling them like cattle. The soldiers had their rifles drawn and they prodded the men and women forward, pushing them to hurry up and move. One elderly woman stumbled and fell heavily onto the ground, crying out in pain. A man, perhaps her husband, rushed to help her up before one of the soldiers could get to her. Children sobbed loudly, but their voices were drowned out by their mothers who wailed even louder.

Paul noted all of this in the periphery of his vision. But his focus was squarely on Analia. Her eyes were downcast, watching the ground and stepping carefully over the debris that littered the sidewalks and road. She clutched the arm of her mother on one side of her, and her father on the other, helping them move forward. When she finally raised her head to look at the synagogue, now fully in flames, she released her father's arm and brought her hand up to her mouth. Even at a distance, Paul could see the horror in her eyes as she realized what was happening. He longed to do something—anything to help her. But he felt as helpless as he had felt the day he saw her cleaning the streets of Düsseldorf.

"Troop leader, what are they doing with those people?" Paul found his voice and turned to Franz.

He looked puzzled. "People? Oh, you mean the Jews. That's what I want everyone to witness." Franz turned and shouted to the other boys who were gathering around him. "Watch how easy it is to get rid of these insects. It's off to the concentration camps with them."

As Franz spoke, a fleet of open-back trucks rolled up beside the synagogue. More police jumped from the backs and rushed over to the Jews, all of whom were standing in shocked silence as they saw their synagogue burning to the ground. It had grown eerily quiet on the street. No more whooping and hollering. No more shattering glass and shouts of glee. All Paul heard was the sound of crackling and sizzling wood from the synagogue that continued to burn like a giant bonfire.

One of the Nazi soldiers barked a sharp order, and the Jews began to run to the trucks, pushed along by soldiers on all sides. Like a river whose dam had broken, the Jews surged forward. More people stumbled. If they fell, they were in danger of being trampled by those coming up behind them. The first group reached a truck and began to climb onboard. More people were pushed up into the open truck—more people than Paul could count. And when the first truck could not possibly hold another person, a second truck pulled up and the Jews were pushed to climb onboard that one.

Paul did not lose sight of Analia, even when the crowd closed her in. She still held tightly to her mother on one arm and her father on the other, trying to obey the Nazi soldiers who were screaming for the Jews to move, push, and climb. The soldiers' shouts joined the sound of the fire, along with the wails that erupted like one giant voice from the throng of Jews.

Suddenly, a soldier rushed forward and grabbed Analia by the arm, yanking her away from her parents who were about to climb onto one of the trucks. The soldier pushed her toward another truck that had pulled up.

"Mama!" Analia shrieked, struggling to free herself from the soldier's grasp. The soldier ignored her cry and pushed her even harder.

That's when Paul knew he had to move.

CHAPTER 23

Wednesday, November 9, 1938, 7:00 p.m.

Keeping his eyes fixed on Analia, Paul sprang forward toward the group of Jews being shoved toward the trucks. He elbowed his way through the crowd, past mothers and fathers, grandparents, and children. Analia was at the front of a cluster of Jews who were all about to get onto one of the trucks. He came up behind her just as she was reaching up to climb on. Paul grabbed her arm and whirled her around.

"Paul!" Analia's face was streaked with tears mixed with soot creating rivers of gray and black that lined her cheeks. In her eyes, there was a look of pain, the degree to which Paul had never seen. All of that turned to fear and confusion when she noted, once again, his Hitler Youth uniform. She stiffened.

There was no time for explanations. Besides, Paul didn't really have one. All he knew was that he needed to get her out of there, and get her out fast.

"Hold on to me," he said, teeth clenched. "Come with me." With that, he pulled her away from the truck and away from the crowd.

Analia resisted and tugged back, trying to wrench herself free of Paul's grasp.

He held on even tighter. "You have to trust me. I'm here to help you. Please," he begged.

A moment passed, and then Analia's eyes softened ever so slightly. But still she fought back against his pull. "My parents!" she screamed, turning her head away from him and scanning the crowd.

Paul looked around just in time to see the truck that held Analia's parents roar off into the smoke-filled night. He could just make out their two figures clutching each other at the back of the truck. Analia followed Paul's gaze and cried out again. The crowd around Paul was still jostling and pushing. Panic filled the air along with screams and cries for help.

"We can't do anything for them," Paul yelled above the deafening noise.

Tears flowed more fiercely down Analia's face as the realization of her parents' fate set in. She squeezed her eyes tightly together, then opened them, and nodded. Her face looked lost, her eyes tortured.

Paul tightened his grip on her arm. There was chaos everywhere, and that gave Paul the opportunity he needed to pull her away from the others. He began to guide her through the crowd, ever aware of the soldiers who kept pushing more Jews onto the trucks. As Paul and Analia emerged into a small clearing, Kiki suddenly appeared in front of him, blocking his way. How had she found him in this mob?

"Are you all right?" she asked.

Paul nodded. That's when Kiki looked over at Analia, seeing her for the first time. Her eyes traveled from Analia's face down to the yellow star on her coat, and then back to Paul. Analia barely acknowledged Kiki. She had become limp next to Paul, numbed by everything that was happening. She slumped against him, hanging her head. Kiki didn't ask any questions. She nodded grimly and leaned closer to Paul.

"We're trying to help some other Jews who managed to get away. Like we did with the Blidners. That's all we can do right now. Get to the beach when you can." She nodded at Analia. "And get her there, too. We'll assemble there after this mess is over." And then she was gone, disappearing into the smoke.

What to do now? Kiki had said to get to the beach, but that was impossible at the moment. The roads would be patrolled; Paul was sure of that. And right now, Analia was in no condition to sneak through the woods or hike the distance to join up with the Pirates. There was only one idea that Paul had—dangerous as he knew it would be. He needed to get Analia to his house. He would hide her there, take a breath, and then think of what to do when this madness had passed.

Even as he pushed forward with Analia next to him, his mind was racing over what he would tell his parents. He'd have to reveal everything about his activities with the Pirates. What would their reaction be? And how much was he risking their safety by including them in all of this? The dangers were great. But everything about this time was dangerous, wasn't it? Besides, what other choice did he have? None!

He would worry about his parents later. Right now, he had to focus on getting Analia out of this area without being seen or caught. Behind him, other boys from the Hitler Youth were still preoccupied with stoking the flames of the fire in the synagogue. He could hear their whoops as they continued to heave rocks and other sharp items up at the building and at other smaller shops and buildings nearby. He had no idea where Harold was; he had lost sight of his friend when he had run up to get Analia. He'd also lost sight of Franz, and he prayed that the troop leader was nowhere nearby.

"Stay close to me," he whispered to Analia as he pulled her along, trying to walk as quickly as possible toward the end of the street.

Just twenty more steps and we'll be away from all of this, Paul thought. He believed that if they could just get around this one corner, they'd be able to slip into some darker shadows and alleys, and he'd find a better route back home. He wrapped his arm around Analia's waist, trying to keep her moving. She felt like dead weight next to him. He knew she was probably in shock. But he couldn't worry about that either. Mama would help take care of her; of that he was certain. But they needed to get off the streets.

Eight more steps; five more; two more. But just as they reached the corner and were about to disappear around it, something made Paul hesitate and turn. And when he looked behind him, his stomach dropped. There was Ernst. He had pulled away from the rest of the Hitler Youth boys and was staring straight in Paul's direction. This time, there was no doubt about it. Ernst could see him, he could see Analia, and from the look on his face, he knew exactly what was happening.

CHAPTER 24

Wednesday, November 9, 1938, 8:00 p.m.

Paul's breath caught in his chest and his heart sank. He was certain that Ernst was going to come after him. At the very least, he would report Paul's desertion to Franz. Paul and Analia needed to get to safety—and fast! But as the two of them rounded the corner, Paul realized that was going to be more dangerous than he had thought. The smaller streets surrounding the synagogue were just as packed with soldiers and police. And on top of that, German citizens of Düsseldorf had joined the crowds, streaming out of their homes to watch as Jewish stores and businesses were ransacked. Some were even joining in, throwing stones, rocks, pipes, and other metal objects at the buildings and cheering as glass windows shattered. Small fires burned everywhere, and the road and sidewalks were littered with garbage, glass, and debris.

Paul had hoped that these surrounding streets would be less chaotic, and that he'd be able to slink home unnoticed with Analia by his side. But looking around he knew that would not be possible. There was only one thing to do, and that was to push forward. He pulled Analia along next to him. She moved as if in a trance, numbly placing one foot in front of the other. Her arms hung limply by her side. Her hair had fallen across her face, which was pale as the moon that kept disappearing behind the plumes of smoke. Her eyes were wide and staring ahead, hollow and unfocused.

Paul still had his arm wrapped around her waist, urging her to move more quickly. The crowd continued to rush in all directions, pushing Paul and Analia first one way, and then the other. No one was paying attention to the two of them; people were more interested in trying to get closer to the action. That, at least, was good. Paul hoped it provided some protection for the two of them and a barrier between himself and the Nazis who continued to patrol the streets. Perhaps in this bedlam, he'd be able to get Analia to his house unnoticed. There were still several blocks to go before he'd feel safe.

"Keep walking, Analia," he urged, feeling her hesitate and stumble. She had not said a word since they had left the trucks, not since she had seen her parents driven away.

A man pushed past Paul and Analia holding a rock in his hands. Without thinking, Paul paused and watched as the man flung the rock toward a small shop. It looked like it might have been a bakery or sweet shop. A Jewish star was painted on its window. The rock hit the star right in its center, cracking the glass and sending thousands of shards, like tiny spikes, splintering toward the ground. That's when Analia cried out again, coming out of her daze as she watched the terrible destruction.

"We have to move," Paul said again. He was just about to resume walking when suddenly, he heard someone call his name.

"Ritter! Stop!"

Paul drew his arm back from Analia's waist and grabbed her arm again. For one frantic moment, he thought it had to be Ernst. His mouth went dry as he froze and felt Analia stiffen next to him. Then he turned his head slowly, exhaling when he saw that it wasn't Ernst, thank goodness! And it wasn't Franz either. It was Max, the smaller boy from his Hitler Youth group who had jumped the fire ahead of Harold that day months ago. Paul was not friends with him, though they regularly saw one another at meetings. Max caught up with Paul.

"What are you doing?" he asked. "Why aren't you with the group?" Max planted his feet on the pavement directly in front of Paul. In the intervening months, he had still not grown into his uniform.

Max stared at Paul, who didn't respond. Then Max turned to look to Analia, his eyes widening as he noted her star. Paul squeezed Analia's arm tightly. She flinched and he quickly loosened his grip.

"What are you doing?" Max asked again. This time, a tinge of wariness crept into his voice.

Paul's mind was going a mile a minute as he struggled to come up with a response. What could he say? How could he possibly get out of this situation? He opened his mouth, sputtered something, and then closed it quickly.

"Why is she with you?" Max asked, more forcefully this time. His eyes narrowed and he moved his feet further apart on the ground.

Paul sucked in quick gulps of air. He could feel his body beginning to shake. But he had to do something. He pulled himself up as tall as he could, and said, "This Jew was separated from the others that were being arrested. Our troop leader told me to take her to the Stadthaus where she'll be imprisoned with some others until she can be taken away." It was a miracle that he'd come up with anything to say. But was it enough? Would Max accept it?

Max still looked suspicious. His eyes traveled from Paul to Analia, back and forth. Paul could sense the doubt radiating off of him like the heat from the fires that blazed all around them.

"Please, please don't take me away. I'll do anything, but please let me go!"

It was Analia talking—pleading. Paul whirled to look her in the eyes. She stared back at him more evenly than he'd seen since he had pulled her away from the synagogue. What was happening? Analia knew he was trying to help her, not turn her in.

"Please don't imprison me. I beg of you!" Analia implored again. She continued to stare at him, and a light went off in his head as he realized what she was trying to do. She had the presence of mind to go along with his story. Where had she found the strength to speak up?

"Quiet!" Paul commanded, playing along with her act. "You'll do as I say."

He turned back to Max. "You have to know how to handle the Jews," he said.

Max paused, still eyeing them both with some doubt. He was just about to open his mouth and say something when another voice called out.

"Paul, I've been looking for you."

Paul turned his head to see Harold striding up the street in their direction. Harold stopped in front of Paul, glancing first at Analia and then at Max. His eyes were remarkably calm; they betrayed nothing.

"Hello, Max," he said. "Why aren't you with the group?"

Max's eyes narrowed even more. "I could ask you the same question, Becker."

"I came to find Paul," Harold replied.

That's when Paul jumped in. "I was telling Max that I was taking this Jew to the Stadthaus, just like the troop leader instructed me to."

Harold paused and his brow creased ever so slightly. But a second later, he nodded and said, "Yes, that's right. That's why I came to find you. The troop leader wanted me to tell you to make sure to get her there as quickly as possible. There's a transport that's going to be leaving soon and he wants her on it."

A moment of relief flowed through Paul as he stared at Harold. His friend's composure and calm in this moment were astonishing. Harold was also playing along, helping Paul just as he'd helped when the Gestapo had come to his house to question him.

"Well, I hate to miss everything that's going on back there," Harold said, turning back to Max. "Did you see the fire?"

Max paused for one more moment, his eyes still on Paul and Analia. And then he turned to Harold, his face relaxing. "It was wonderful, wasn't it? The greatest fire I've ever seen."

"We'll teach the Jews who's in charge now, won't we?"

Harold said, throwing an arm around Max's shoulder.

Paul couldn't believe the words that were coming out of Harold's mouth. And he couldn't believe how self-assured Harold sounded—how easily and courageously he was performing.

"We're all going to head to another synagogue after this one and light it up as well," Harold continued. "You don't want to miss that, do you?"

By now, Max's face was glowing, and he was grinning from ear to ear. "Of course not! This is a glorious night—a night to remember. I'm coming with you." He glanced back at Paul.

"I guess you have things under control," he said pointing at Analia.

"Absolutely!" Paul said, swallowing hard. "I'll catch up with you once I've deposited this Jew in jail, where she belongs."

Analia whimpered once more as if to stress her supposed helplessness.

That seemed to satisfy Max. "Heil Hitler!" he proclaimed, raising his arm.

"Heil Hitler!" Paul replied. The words nearly choked him.

Harold turned, and with his arm still around Max's shoulder, the two began to march back toward the big synagogue. Only when they had gone a few steps did Harold glance back over his shoulder. His mouth was set in a determined line. His eyes caught Paul's and he nodded a quick acknowledgment. Then, he turned back and continued to walk away.

Paul felt his legs go weak. Analia slumped next to him as if the effort of the last few minutes had finally done her in. He quickly encircled her waist again, holding her up as he turned her toward his house.

Shakily, he said, "We're nearly there."

CHAPTER 25

Wednesday, November 9, 1938, 9:00 p.m.

The lights were out in Paul's house when he and Analia finally crept up the walkway and approached the door. The darkened house didn't surprise Paul. He imagined that his parents were sitting somewhere inside, probably in a back bedroom, as far from the street as possible, with the radio on, and listening closely to the news. He hoped that the pitch-black house would ensure that no one would pay attention to them and come pounding at the door.

Paul turned the key in the lock and pushed the door open, first glancing around to make sure no prying eyes from any nosy neighbors were watching him. The only neighbor to really worry about was Ernst, and Paul knew for certain that he wasn't home. If anything, he might be somewhere reporting that he'd seen Paul and a Jewish girl making a getaway. For now, the coast seemed to be clear. He pushed Analia through the door and closed it behind them.

"Paul? Is that you?" Mama's anxious voice greeted him in the dark.

Still holding Analia's arm, he followed the sound into the bedroom near the back of the house. Even before he got there, he could already hear a radio announcer proclaiming that a great event had taken place in Düsseldorf and in cities and towns across Germany. Synagogues, Jewish shops, Jewish schools—all had been torched and their windows shattered. "Thousands of Jews have been arrested," the announcer continued. "This is a victory for our Führer, and a step toward ridding Germany of its Jews. The destruction tonight was magnificent and complete!" the announcer proclaimed. Paul didn't need to hear anymore; he had seen it all.

He entered the bedroom to find his parents as expected, perched on the end of their bed, huddled next to the radio. One small lamp cast a dusky yellow glow in the otherwise darkened room. His parents rose from the bed to greet him, a look of relief splashed across their faces. The look disappeared instantly as Paul pulled Analia into the room next to him. They immediately recognized her.

Mama sank back down onto the bed. Papa reached over to turn down the volume on the radio. He continued to stand, staring at Paul and then at Analia. "Paul," he stuttered. "What…what is this?"

Paul held one hand out in front of him to stop his parents from saying anything else. "Mama, Papa, I need to talk to both of you. There's a lot I have to say, and I don't think I have much time. So please, listen to me."

His parents' faces were as pale as Analia's. She had her head down—not raising her eyes to look at Paul's parents. Her hands were clasped in front of her.

Paul began to talk quickly, starting with the day he had gone to the beach and had been introduced to the Edelweiss Pirates. He talked about how he had decided that he needed to join them, particularly after the time that he and the Hitler Youth were marched into town to supervise the Jews who were forced to clean the streets of Düsseldorf. He felt Analia shudder next to him when he explained all that. Next, he talked about the raids he had gone on with the Pirates, including the one that had resulted in the Gestapo coming to question him here in the house. When he mentioned stealing food from the warehouse and leaving it for Analia and her family, that was when her eyes shot up to meet his.

"That was you? You're the one who brought us food?" Analia asked in surprise.

Paul stared back at her, nodded, and continued

talking. His father tried to question him a couple of times, but Paul pleaded with him to let him continue. Papa sat back on the bed. He reached a hand out to grab Mama's, squeezing it tightly for support. Paul described being on the streets with the Hitler Youth earlier in the night and being ordered to throw rocks at the burning synagogue.

"There were hundreds of Jewish people being arrested and taken away, right under our noses. And then I saw Analia." Paul turned to look at her. She was staring at him now. Tears were gathering in the corners of her eyes. "I managed to get her away from all that," Paul continued. "This was the only place I could think of to bring her."

The only sound in the room was the low buzz of indistinguishable voices coming from the radio: the muted noise of a roaring crowd. Papa reached over and quickly shut the radio off. The room became dead silent.

At first, in the stillness of the bedroom, Paul couldn't tell what his parents were thinking. For a brief moment, he was terrified that they might turn him away, or insist that he hand Analia over to the Nazi authorities! But they were the ones who had always told him to treat everyone equally, no matter what their religion or background. *Don't forget who you really are.* Mama's words had rung in Paul's ears every minute that he had been forced to take part in the activities of the Hitler Youth.

Mama was the one who finally broke the tense silence. She walked up to Analia and reached out to take her hands. "What about your parents, dear?" she asked.

Analia looked into Mama's eyes and shook her head. That's when the tears began to flow freely down her cheeks. They were the first tears Paul had seen since her parents had been put on the truck.

Mama sighed and embraced Analia, pulling her into her arms. Analia's body heaved and trembled as she finally released her pain and fear and sobbed heavily on Mama's shoulder. No one stopped her. Her sobs echoed in the room. It took a long time for them to turn to sniffles, and then to hiccups, until her breathing became even, and it was quiet once more. Only then, did Mama stand back to look at her.

"Come," Mama said. "Let me get you some tea." She looked over at Paul. "I think we all could do with some."

"Mama, there's no time for…." His voice trailed off when he saw the determined look in his mother's eyes.

"Please don't argue with me, Paul. This girl needs something to eat and drink. And so do you."

There was still so much that Paul needed to do—needed to figure out. But the truth was, he was exhausted. All he really wanted to do was crawl into his room, into his bed, pull the covers over his head and sleep until the world had returned to normal. In that moment, he was unable to argue with his mother. He followed her numbly into the kitchen. Papa followed along as well. Mama was still holding Analia's hand and she guided her to a kitchen chair. Paul slumped down in one next to her.

Within minutes, Mama set cups of steaming tea in front of Paul and Analia, accompanied by plates of bread and cheese. Analia reached out to pick up her cup and take a sip. Swirls of steam rose around her face. She looked up at Paul.

"I want to tell you what happened tonight," she said.

Paul had been longing to ask but hadn't been able to find a way. "You don't have to," he said.

"I want to." She looked up at Paul's parents. "You need to know just how awful this is. You need to know what the Nazis are doing to Jews." The fear and sadness of the night seemed to have faded in Analia, replaced with a calm resolve and firmness.

Everyone stared at Analia—Paul, Papa, Mama. Paul's stomach was in knots. As much as he wanted to know the details of what had happened to the Jews in the city, he dreaded hearing these facts. Analia finally took a deep breath and began to talk.

"We could hear them in the streets tonight—even before dark. And we were expecting something; we didn't know what. But after the report of the shooting of vom Rath, we knew the Nazis were going to come after us. My parents turned out the lights." She glanced again at Paul's parents. "Just like you did tonight. But it didn't do any good. We heard them pounding on our door and, when no one went to answer, they just broke it down."

Analia's voice trailed off as the memories swept over her. She shook her head from side to side, trying to clear her thoughts. A moment later, she continued, her voice stronger now. "Four of them came in. One carried an axe; the others had guns. The one with the axe started to hack our furniture into pieces—our chairs, lamps, paintings, the large wardrobe that had been my grandmother's, passed down to my mother. One of the others pulled the curtains down from our windows and threw dishes onto the floor, smashing them to pieces. A third one heaved our clothes and blankets and feather pillows out the window and onto the sidewalk. There was a cake that my mother had managed to bake with the last bit of our flour and sugar. It was meant for a birthday celebration for my papa." A brief smile passed over Analia's lips and then vanished as quickly as it had appeared. "One of the soldiers saw the cake, picked it up, threw it onto the floor, and then stomped his boot into the middle of it."

"What did you do?" Paul choked out the question.

Analia shook her head. "What could we do? Nothing. We just stood huddled together, holding on to each other, and hoping it would all end quickly. Hoping they would finish their destruction and then leave us alone." She stared at Paul, her eyes full of hatred. "We would have figured something out if they'd just left us alone. But that didn't happen."

Paul gulped. He knew what was coming. "Instead, they rounded you up and marched you out the door."

Analia nodded. "Yes. There was a long line of Jews already gathered outside, so many of our friends and neighbors. We knew that the same thing must have happened to them, that the Nazis had been moving from house to house, destroying everyone's property. A couple of the men had bruises on their faces. The Nazis must have been particularly rough with them. We didn't want to get hurt, so we didn't resist. We were pushed into the line with everyone else and marched to the synagogue. We could see it burning." She looked up again at Paul. "You know the rest."

Silence fell on the room once more. Mama finally spoke. "Your coat is torn," she said.

Paul hadn't even noticed the rip in Analia's coat—a long tear just above her yellow star. The star had folded over and hung down from only a couple of threads, as if it too had been wounded. Analia reached up to touch it as if she hadn't realized anything had happened either.

"Come with me," Mama continued. "Whatever happens, you're going to need something else to wear. I'll find you something."

With that, Analia stood and followed Mama from the room.

Paul was left alone with his father.

CHAPTER 26

Wednesday, November 9, 1938, 10:00 p.m.

Papa's eyes wandered around the kitchen, his eyes landing on Paul. It was as if he were searching for something to say or advise—anything to break the tension and uncertainty that clung to every corner of the room. Paul had never seen his father look so distressed. A line of sweat dotted his forehead and upper lip. He reached into his pocket, withdrew a handkerchief and, with a trembling hand, wiped the sweat away.

"The Jews they arrested tonight, they're taking them away to the concentration camps." Paul filled his father in on what Franz had told the Hitler Youth when they had all stood in front of the burning synagogue. That moment seemed ages ago. Was it only a few hours that had passed?

Papa swallowed hard, the sweat reappearing across his forehead. "What are you going to do?"

Ever since he had spotted Analia in front of the burning synagogue, Paul's mind had been racing, trying to figure that out. There was only one idea that he kept coming back to.

"I'm going to take Analia to the Pirates." Kiki's message—*get to the beach*—had resonated in Paul's mind. Kiki said that the Pirates were trying to help some other Jews who had managed to slip away from the crowd. Paul didn't know what had happened to the Blidner family and little Stella. He had no idea if a safe hiding place had been found for them. He prayed it had. He hoped that the Pirates had some plan for how to get this new group of Jews to safety. And that they would be able to do the same for Analia. He told all of this to his father. "I'm sure they'll know where to keep her safe." Paul didn't feel nearly as confident as he hoped he sounded.

"And you?" Papa asked in barely a whisper. "Will you be safe?"

That was the other question that was plaguing Paul. He had been spotted by Ernst. He had been questioned by Max. Surely by now, one or both of those boys had reported him to Franz who would have already noticed his absence. Franz was no fool. He would have figured out that Paul had deserted the group in favor of helping a Jewish girl. That was treason and punishable with arrest or something even worse. Paul's cover had been blown. There was no going back, no way to recover from this. His only hope now was that Harold was going to be able to figure out a way to get out from under the mess he had put himself in by lying for Paul.

"I don't think I'm going to be safe living here anymore," he said to his father. Papa looked away. "I'm going to seek shelter with the Pirates as well—at least for the time being."

"For how long?" Papa croaked the question out.

"I don't know. For a while, I think. For as long as it takes to get through this terrible time."

Papa nodded sadly. "You're so young…," he began, and then faltered.

"I'm nearly sixteen," Paul replied trying to sound strong. The truth was he felt so much older than that. After everything that had happened in the last day, in the last weeks and months, Paul felt ancient—like someone who had lived a hundred lives. "I guess the good news is that I'm not going to have to lie anymore," Paul said. "Not to them, and not to myself." That part was true. Kiki had told him that he needed to stay silent and pretend he was one of the Hitler Youth in order to keep safe and to work with the Pirates in any way that was needed. *When the time is right, you'll break the silence*, she had said. Well, the time was now, Paul realized.

"You're the one who told me I had to be true to myself, Papa," Paul said. "You taught me that; you and Mama."

Papa exhaled a long and aching breath. "I just didn't imagine anything like this. Let me tell your mother," he added. "I think it will be easier coming from me."

He turned and left the room. A moment later, Analia walked in. She had washed her face and combed her hair that was now tied at the back of her head with a dark ribbon. Paul recognized the coat that she was wearing—a long brown one that his mother used to wear. "It fits you," he said.

A small smile passed across Analia's face. She reached her hand up to her heart and the place where a yellow star had been sewn to her old coat. Then, she quickly withdrew her hand. "It feels so strange not to have a star there."

Paul frowned. "You and the others shouldn't have to wear them in the first place. That is wrong, along with so many other things."

"The day we were ordered to clean the streets and I saw you, I was so angry. I thought you were one of them. I should have known better." Analia paused. "Your parents have been so kind. And so have you. I don't know what would have happened tonight if you hadn't...." She stopped and stared at Paul. "You've always been a good friend. I should have known that." Then, she walked over to him and wrapped her arms around his neck, holding tightly. "Thank you."

Paul returned the hug, feeling her cheek against his, and her hair next to his eyes. He wanted to stand there longer. He wanted to feel the warmth of that hug forever. But after only a moment, he pulled her arms away and stepped back. "We need to go," he said. And then, he quickly explained where he was taking her—to the beach and to the Pirates. As he talked, his mother and father reentered the kitchen. Mama's eyes were red and ringed with tears. Papa held her with one arm wrapped around her shoulder.

"I need to make you some sandwiches," Mama insisted, sniffling loudly.

Paul glanced at the clock, ticking on the wall above the stove. His mother caught his look. "Neither of you ate the food I put out earlier. I won't let you go without making some sandwiches for you to take with you. Who knows how long it will be before you eat again?"

Paul glanced at the clock. They had been here long enough—longer than was safe. The urgency to leave was weighing on him, like a heavy bag cutting into his shoulders. He was just about to say that to his parents when there was a sudden and persistent knock at the door.

Analia's face went white, and she whispered, "They found us!"

CHAPTER 27
Wednesday, November 9, 1938, 10:30 p.m.

Paul brought a finger up to his lips to quiet everyone. Mama's eyes met his and quickly wiped away the trace of her tears. Papa raised a shaky hand to wipe the sweat from his brow. Paul motioned for his father to go and answer the door. Papa straightened his vest and buttoned the top button. Then he pulled his shoulders back and nodded at Paul. The pounding at the front door resumed for a second time.

Just before his father went to answer the door, Paul grabbed Analia by the arm and pulled her into a closet just outside the kitchen. For a moment, she had that same stunned look on her face—the same numb stare that she'd had when Paul had grabbed her away from the trucks. But a second later, she shook her head, clearing the shock away, and quickly crouched next to Paul in the closet.

Paul kept the door open a crack just so that he could hear what was going on. A sliver of light from the kitchen kept the small space from descending into complete blackness. He squatted down onto the floor, Analia next to him. A broom pressed into his back and a bucket for mopping was jammed against his shoulder. He was breathing in quick shallow gulps. His chest rose and fell, and the muscles in his neck bulged and strained as if he was drowning. The sound of his breathing was raspy and wheezy, like wind rushing through tall grass. And it was loud, a sound that might be heard by whoever was knocking at the door. Seeing his panic, Analia took control, placing her hand in front of Paul's face, moving it up and down in a slow counting rhythm as if she were conducting an orchestra, helping him slow and then silence his panting. His eyes followed her hand and within seconds, his breathing had eased and quieted. He glanced over at her, nodding gratefully.

The pounding at the front door persisted. Paul heard his father call out, "Yes, yes, I'm coming. One moment, please."

Another pause, and then the sound of steps moving out of the kitchen and toward the front of the house. As soon as the front door creaked open, Paul recognized the voice of the Gestapo officer, the same one who had come to question him before. Paul strained forward eager to hear what was being said.

"Herr Ritter," a click of heels. "We've come looking for your son."

Papa spoke. "My son? Well, he's certainly not here."

"Where is he?"

"With his youth group, of course." This time, it was Mama speaking. She sounded astonishingly calm and sure of herself. A moment earlier, she had been crying and near a breaking point. Paul marveled at how she had managed to pull herself together so quickly.

"We've been listening to the radio," Mama continued. "Hearing the reports of the glorious destruction of all those synagogues and Jewish stores. We assumed Paul's Hitler Youth group would be right there in the middle of it all, helping wherever they could."

A pause and then, "You think he's with his youth division?"

"Of course," Mama said. "Where else would he be on this night when all of Germany is declaring its allegiance to the Führer?"

Another pause, this one longer than the last. Paul imagined that the Gestapo officer was staring his parents up and down—trying to detect a hesitation, a falter, pause, or waver in their assertion.

"We've heard some reports about your son's behavior that are somewhat disturbing. We think he may be helping a Jew," the officer continued. His voice had become sharper and more adamant, increasing in volume.

When Paul glanced over at Analia, he could read the pure anger on her face. She pressed closer to him and lay her head on his shoulder.

"I have no idea what you're talking about." This time Papa answered the officer. "Our son is loyal to Germany as are we."

"I'm only telling you about our report. Your son appears to be missing."

"And you think he's here?" Mama asked. "Why, we would never give him that kind of protection—especially if he is doing something illegal."

Once again, Paul marveled at his parents' ability to respond so convincingly. He pressed his eyes together and leaned forward once more.

Papa responded. "You searched our home before and found nothing. But if you think we have anything to hide, you are most welcome to come in and look around again. We're here to help in any way."

The hairs on Paul's arm stood at attention and a cold sweat began to travel down his back. Adrenaline coursed through his veins. What was his father thinking? What was he doing, inviting them in? Analia pressed even closer to him.

This time, the pause was unbearable as Paul waited to

hear if the Gestapo would enter the house and begin to search. He knew that he and Analia would be discovered within minutes. Their fate would be sealed along with the fate of his parents. He braced himself and wrapped his arm around Analia's shoulder.

Finally, the Gestapo officer spoke. "We have too much to do to waste more time here. We trust you to contact us the moment you hear anything, or your son is in touch with you. You must demonstrate your loyalty to Germany and the Führer!"

"Of course," Papa replied.

"The moment we hear anything," Mama added. "We would never tolerate our son engaging in any subversive activities."

One more interminable pause, as if the Gestapo officer was studying Mama and Papa one last time. Finally, the loud snap of boot heels being clicked together again, a harsh pronouncement of "Heil Hitler!" And then the door closed.

A moment later, the closet door creaked open.

CHAPTER 28

Wednesday, November 9, 1938, 11:00 p.m.

Paul stood up on shaky legs and pulled Analia up beside him. She blinked and shielded her eyes against the glare of the kitchen light as Paul guided her out of the closet.

Papa did not waste a second. "We may have bought you a few minutes. But that's all. You have to leave," he said. "Now!"

Paul nodded. "I know. We heard it all." He glanced at Analia whose face was set in a firm stare.

Mama had already turned away and rummaged through the small refrigerator. "I'm still going to make some sandwiches for you."

She stared back at Paul, almost challenging him to try and object. He started to open his mouth and then stopped. There was no point in arguing with his mother.

He knew that she needed to do something, anything to feel useful and to distract herself from the fear that must have been surging through her body—fear for Paul, for Analia, and for herself and Papa. Besides, Paul needed a few minutes to collect some things from his bedroom—sweaters, an extra pair of trousers, socks. He had no idea when he'd be back home.

Analia followed him into his bedroom, sinking down onto the foot of his bed while he pulled a knapsack from his closet and began to stuff it with clothing, a notebook, an extra pair of shoes. He opened the top drawer of his desk and dug underneath his papers to find his Edelweiss pin, staring at it for a second before placing it on the top of the items in his knapsack.

"I'm scared," Analia said softly.

Paul paused from his packing. "I am too."

He had to admit that he'd been afraid since the day he'd joined the Edelweiss Pirates—probably before that, from the time he'd been forced to sign up for the Hitler Youth. But fear could be a good thing, he realized. Kiki had said that nerves kept you sharp. And she was right. They would need all that sharpness in the days to come.

"I'm prepared for whatever I need to do," Analia added. "But I don't want to put you in any more danger."

Paul paused. "I don't want you to worry about me. You need to think about yourself. I know that the Pirates will do everything they possibly can to keep you safe until they can get you out of the country or to some other hiding place. And I'll be right there with you."

Paul hoped he sounded convincing. The truth was, he had no idea what the Pirates would be able to do for Analia, or how they would keep her safe. For that matter, he wasn't even sure how he was going to be able to stay with them—to live in the forest, to engage in dangerous activities all the time, to be a criminal in the eyes of the Nazi government, to never see his home or his parents. He hadn't allowed himself the chance to really think about any of the details. Leaving home to join the Pirates in the woods was something he knew he had to do. But it came with so many unknowns.

Analia smiled faintly. "And my parents? What do you think will happen to them?"

Paul couldn't even begin to answer that question—not for Analia's parents, or for the other Jewish people who had been hauled away in Düsseldorf, or for Jews across the country that were also probably being arrested as they spoke.

"Maybe your group can do something to try and look for them?" Analia asked. The desperation in her voice was painful to hear.

Paul didn't want to take away her hope—pointless as it probably was. He knew that hope was as important as fear when it came to surviving and Analia would need that in the days to come. But he also didn't want to lie to her. Instead, he said, "I have to believe that countries all around the world are going to hear about what happened across Germany tonight. They'll hear about synagogues and stores being ransacked and Jewish people being taken away. And hopefully when other countries hear about all that, they'll condemn Hitler. They'll overthrow him, so that he and his followers can't do any more harm. That will be your parents' best chance. I have to believe that...." His voice trailed off. He wasn't sure he believed it himself.

Analia looked away and sighed. "Do you remember that time when we went to the beach—when we were still in school together?"

Paul had never forgotten it.

Analia looked up. "That seems so long ago, as though it never happened. Life was so much easier then. Easier and happier."

Paul nodded, unable to talk.

"Do you think we'll ever go back to being happy?"

He wasn't sure how to answer that either. "I hope so," he finally said.

At that moment, Mama knocked on the door and entered carrying a bag of sandwiches. Paul accepted them gratefully. Mama also had a few sweaters and blouses for Analia.

"You need clothes as well," she said.

Paul placed them in the knapsack along with the

sandwiches. Then he pulled the drawstrings together. He slipped into a warm jacket, hoisted the pack onto his shoulders, and held his hand out to Analia. Together, they followed Mama out of his room and to the front door where Papa was already waiting. Paul faced his parents.

"I'll try to be in touch with you—or get word to you. But I don't know when I'll see…." He didn't finish— couldn't get the words out of his mouth for fear that he'd break down.

Mama hugged him tightly. "We are so proud of you, and everything that you're doing." Her voice quivered. "Just stay safe."

Papa reached out to shake Paul's hand, and then pulled him into a hug as well. When Paul finally stepped back, he could see the tears flowing freely down his father's face. Paul realized with a start that it was probably the only time he'd ever seen Papa cry. He swallowed hard, staring into his parents' faces, trying to memorize every line, every shadow, the dimple in his father's cheek, the freckles across the bridge of his mother's nose.

His parents each stepped forward to hug Analia. "We'll think of you every minute, my dear," Mama said. "And hope you'll be safe."

Finally, Paul opened the door and looked up and down the darkened street. Then, he glanced back at his parents one last time. Taking a deep breath, he reached for Analia's hand. She grabbed it, squeezing it tightly, and together they walked into the night.

EPILOGUE

Saturday, November 9, 1946

Eight Years Later

Paul rushed through the streets of Düsseldorf, eager to get home. His classes had gone later than usual, and now he feared that he might be late. He turned the collar of his coat up to his ears and pulled his wool scarf tighter around his neck as he jogged along, dodging pedestrians, children, and dogs. The Königsallee was busy, teeming with citizens shopping on the boulevard. Men in suits walked at a brisk pace, mothers carried shopping bags while they pushed their babies in carriages, and young children strolled, lingering in front of store windows until the owners came out and insisted they move on.

Paul stopped at a bakery to pick up some cakes, glancing again at his watch. The baker was working slowly, wanting to package the torte just right. Paul didn't care if it was thrown into a box. He needed to get home quickly. Bag finally in hand, he turned up a side street that took him into what had once been the Jewish section of Düsseldorf. Up ahead were the burned-out remains of the New Synagogue. Paul paused for the briefest of seconds as he always did when he went by this place. With a start, he realized that today was November 9—the eight-year anniversary of that terrible night when the synagogue and surrounding businesses had been looted and set on fire. That night had come to be known as Kristallnacht—the night of broken glass, an apt name for the destruction that had taken place. Paul had thought that the terrible events of that night would alert surrounding countries to Hitler's madness. He had believed that the world would rise up against that evil man. He couldn't have been more wrong. Less than a year after that night, Hitler had invaded Poland to set off a world war resulting in millions of deaths, including six million Jews murdered across Europe. The war had lasted six long years, from 1939 to 1945.

Paul glanced once more over his shoulder at the ruins of the synagogue. He hoped it would be restored one day, but so far nothing was happening. Turning one last corner, he finally approached the apartment building where he now lived, trying to shrug off the images of war and destruction. He bounded up the stairs to his apartment on the third floor, turned the key in the lock, and opened the door, looking down at his watch once more. Thank goodness he had gotten home in time.

He was just beginning to place the desserts on a platter when there was a knock at the door. It was still too early, he thought as he ran to open it. Kiki was on the other side. She hugged him as she came through the door.

"I tried to get here as soon as I could."

He returned the hug and stepped back to stare at her. They had fought side by side as members of the Edelweiss Pirates throughout the war, continuing to thwart the efforts of the Nazis whenever and wherever they could. They had continued to paint anti-Nazi slogans on buildings and distribute pamphlets. But they had also moved on to raiding army campsites and stealing guns and explosives. There had been too many close calls to even count, so many times when a member of the Pirates had almost been captured or shot. It was a miracle that both Paul and Kiki had survived it all.

Not all of the Pirates had been as lucky. Many were arrested and put in prison. Luka had been captured again, this time during a raid of the Pirates' campsite. No one knew who had revealed their hiding spot. By the time the soldiers surrounded them, only a few Pirates had managed to get away safely. Luka was taken in for questioning, but this time he was not released. After several weeks, he was hanged in the same courtyard that the Nazis had shown him after his first arrest. There had been no trial, no opportunity for Luka to try to defend himself. Just a quick and brutal execution. Kiki had taken the death of her brother very hard. And Paul had been there to comfort her and help her through her pain and grief.

Over time, Paul and Kiki had gone from being comrades to friends to close companions and confidantes. And they remained close friends even after the war had finally ended.

Kiki followed Paul into the kitchen. "Hard day?" she asked.

He nodded. "The usual. We've started going into the hospitals to observe some surgeries. I can't wait until I can watch less and do more."

She smiled. "Always the impatient one."

After the war, Paul had finished his high school requirements in record time so that he could enter university and begin his pre-med studies. His parents had never looked happier than the day he announced he wanted to follow in their professional footsteps. Well, maybe the day he reappeared on the doorstep of their home—that was perhaps the happiest day. He had so little communication with them during the war years, just the occasional note delivered by a comrade.

"And what about you?" Paul asked. "How was your day?"

Kiki was teaching in an elementary school. She usually spent Saturdays like this one preparing her lessons for the week and her mind for the chaos of working with little children. But she said that it made her happy to educate young kids and teach them tolerance for each other—*creating loving hearts*, is what she called it.

"It was a good day. I got a lot done. I'll tell you all about it. By the way, have you heard from Harold lately?"

Paul smiled and nodded at the mention of his good friend. They had reconnected after the war ended. It was then that Paul had discovered that Harold had managed to avoid any trouble with Franz and the Hitler Youth after that fateful night. Paul didn't know how Harold had talked himself out of any serious consequences, and Harold hadn't wanted to say too much about it. Paul always knew that Harold was more resourceful and more courageous than just about anyone he knew.

But that terrible night in the city had settled it for Harold. He knew he couldn't stay in Germany. He was a thinker, not a fighter. In 1939, just before the start of the war, he and his family had managed to get out of the country. They spent the war years in England and stayed there when it was over. Harold was the one who had tracked Paul down at the end of the war. Paul was happily surprised the day the telephone rang and it was

Harold on the other end. Now, they called each other at least once a month and wrote long letters in between. The long-distance calls between London and Düsseldorf were expensive, but they were worth it to the two old friends.

"Did you pick up the desserts?" Kiki asked.

Paul pointed at the platter on the counter. "One poppy seed cake and three jelly donuts. Is it enough?"

"Plenty. You'll have leftovers. I have a feeling you and your guest will do more talking than eating."

At the word "guest," Paul's heart rate quickened. He had imagined, dreamed, and prayed for this day. Closing his eyes, he thought back to the night he and Analia had run from the city to the Pirates' campsite. Getting there had been a nightmare, almost as terrifying as getting Analia away from the burning synagogue and to his house. Roads in and out of the city were patrolled by Nazi vehicles. Soldiers were everywhere. Paul and Analia had hidden in the shadows of buildings and behind trees until they finally made it.

Kiki was already at the campsite, along with Luka and other Pirates. There were also two other Jewish people; a young man and young woman who had broken away from the mass of Jews being arrested in town. The next hours passed in a blur. Luka made plans for Analia and the other two. The refugees would be hidden in a barn. From there, they would be moved to a safe house, and then another, until they could be smuggled out of the country. Paul knew nothing of the details. All he remembered was the frantic good-bye between himself and Analia.

"Will I see you again?" Analia had asked when they parted, eyes brimming with tears.

"I don't know. I hope so."

"Just stay safe."

"You too."

"Thank you, for everything. I'm sorry I ever doubted you."

Then, a quick hug. Paul tried desperately not to let his own tears blur his vision. And then she was gone. The letter that had arrived in his apartment weeks earlier was the first time Paul had heard any news that she had survived.

Somehow, she had managed to hike through Germany and cross into France, traveling through dangerous forests where Nazis patrolled with their vicious dogs. She had begged for food and places to sleep. That was risky as well because civilians were rewarded for delivering Jews to the Nazi authorities. Despite all the dangers, she had managed to cross the border of France into Switzerland. And that's where she had remained for the duration of the war. And now she was coming to visit—and on the eighth anniversary of the night that had changed everything.

"What time did I tell you she was going to be here?" Paul asked Kiki, watching as she rearranged the cake and donuts on the serving dish.

Kiki laughed. "As if you can't remember. You've read that letter from her at least thirty times since it arrived. You know she'll be here any minute."

Paul felt his face redden. Kiki laughed again and reached over to jab him playfully in the arm. "I know what she meant to you." She paused. "Maybe, still means to you?"

Paul looked away. "She was probably my first love. We were so young and naïve." He shook his head. "And then, we had to grow up so fast."

"We all did," Kiki added.

"After that, there was no time for anything else—just survival. But maybe now…." His voice trailed off.

Just then, there was a knock at the door. Paul felt his heartbeat quicken again.

"You ready?" Kiki asked.

Paul nodded and walked over to the door. Taking a deep breath, he opened it.

She had the same rounded cheeks tinged with red as if she had been running to get here. Her long brown hair was pulled back off her face and held in a clip at the back of her head. Her hazel eyes were lit with some sadness and lined around the corners as if she had witnessed too much sorrow in the intervening years.

But on seeing Paul, she smiled, and in that moment, she became the young girl she had once been. There was no mistaking that face.

It was Analia.

AUTHOR'S NOTE

While all the characters in this book are fictional, the story is based on real events. Here are some of those important pieces of history.

Propaganda

When Adolf Hitler took power in Germany in 1933, he created the Ministry of Public Enlightenment and Propaganda. Its goal was to spread the policy of racial antisemitism across Germany, which affected art, music, theater, film, as well as educational material. Children grew up reading racist literature, chanting Nazi-inspired slogans, and attending national rallies. Books like *The Poisonous Mushroom* and *The Poisonous Serpent* were used to brainwash young people into believing that Jews were inferior, evil, and should be despised, and eventually "eliminated." False Nazi propaganda extended even to the very young.

The Hitler Youth

The Hitler Youth was formed in 1926 to train young boys, between the ages of ten and seventeen, to prepare them for service as soldiers in the Nazi army. By the time the Second World War began, there were more than 5.4 million boys who were members. The Nazis shaped the beliefs, thinking, and actions of German youth through the Hitler Youth movement, and its female parallel, the League of German Girls. Young German teens participated in mass rallies, sports and outdoor activities, and marches, all designed to glorify Adolf Hitler and his Nazi party. Young people were urged to turn in anyone, even a family member, who spoke out against Hitler, and to turn against Jewish people and other "inferior" races. This was all false propaganda.

Kristallnacht

Kristallnacht, or the Night of Broken Glass, was a series of violent antisemitic attacks which took place across Germany and Austria on November 9 and 10, 1938. The alleged reason for Kristallnacht was the murder of a German official, Ernst vom Rath, at the hands of a young Jewish teen, Herschel Grynszpan. Grynszpan had sought out and shot vom Rath after his own parents had been arrested and sent to concentration camps. The Nazis vowed revenge. Over the course of two days, Jewish homes, hospitals, and schools were ransacked. Synagogues and businesses were set on fire and destroyed. An estimated 30,000 Jewish people were arrested and sent to concentration camps. The name "Kristallnacht" comes from the shards of broken glass that littered the streets after the windows of Jewish-owned stores, buildings, and synagogues were smashed.

The Edelweiss Pirates

The Edelweiss Pirates, or *Edelweisspiraten* as they were known in German, were a loosely organized group of teenage resistance fighters in Nazi Germany, both girls and boys, between the ages of fourteen and seventeen. Named for the pins and badges in the shape of an Edelweiss flower that members wore on their collars, these teens became one of the largest youth groups that opposed Nazi activities. They came mostly from working class families and saw themselves in opposition to the Hitler Youth. They refused to follow the rules set out by the Nazis and rejected everything to do with Nazi ideas and propaganda. Edelweiss Pirate groups were established in numerous cities across Germany: Cologne, Hamburg, Leipzig, Frankfurt, and Düsseldorf. In each city, they went by slightly different names, such

The Edelweiss Pirates

as *Fahrhtenstenze* (Traveling Dudes), *Kittelbach* Pirates, and *Navajos*. But all considered themselves Edelweiss Pirates.

At first, their intention was to distance themselves from the Hitler Youth. They met in parks and cafés. They took hikes and went on camping trips together. They carried guitars and sang protest songs. Even these innocent activities were considered subversive by the Nazi government and would have been enough to get members arrested.

Over the course of the Second World War, the activities of the Edelweiss Pirates became more defiant and dangerous. They offered shelter to German army deserters, escaped prisoners from concentration camps, and escapees from forced labor camps. They made armed raids on military depots, stole explosives, and supplied them to resistance groups. They distributed anti-Nazi pamphlets and deliberately sabotaged the efforts of the army. Those who were caught were sent to prison or labor camps; some were hanged.

For example, at the age of seventeen, Gertrud Koch refused to join the League of German Girls and instead joined the Edelweiss Pirates. She participated in armed raids on Nazi bases and distributed anti-Hitler leaflets. She was arrested, brutally interrogated, and thrown into prison. She was eventually released. Other Pirates were not so lucky. At the age of fifteen, Jean Julich

Bartholomaeus (Barthel) Schink

was a member of the *Ehrenfelder Navajo* group of the Edelweiss Pirates. After taking part in a plan to blow up the Gestapo headquarters in Cologne, Jean was arrested, held in solitary confinement without trial, and tortured for four months. His friend and fellow Pirate, sixteen-year-old Bartholomaeus (Barthel) Schink, was publicly hanged in Cologne in 1944 for being part of that same plan to blow up the Gestapo headquarters.

In total, there were an estimated 5,000 members of the Edelweiss Pirates from cities across Germany. In 1988, the Edelweiss Pirates were recognized as Righteous Among the Nations, the highest honor that Israel bestows on an individual or a group that aided Jews during the Holocaust.

ACKNOWLEDGMENTS

Of the more than twenty-five books I've written, this is my fourteenth book published by Second Story Press. I cherish my partnership with SSP and with Margie Wolfe, its extraordinary publisher. Margie has become so much more than a publisher. She is a mentor, advisor, and friend. She has never wavered in her support of my writing and in her commitment to Holocaust literature. I'm so grateful for all of it.

This is also one of many books I've written that has been edited by Sarah Silberstein Swartz. I know I've become a better writer thanks to her encouragement and insightful feedback. And her keen attention to every detail has been tremendously helpful. Thanks as well to Melissa Kaita for the beautiful design, and to all the staff at SSP who promote my books with such enthusiasm.

To my beautiful family, my husband, Ian Epstein, my children, Gabi Epstein and Jake Epstein, along with their fabulous partners, Vanessa Smythe and Jeremy Lapalme—I love you. I love that you value and appreciate my writing, I love your ongoing words of encouragement and support. Thank you for it all!

And now, on to writing more stories!

ABOUT THE AUTHOR

KATHY KACER's books have won a number of awards, including the Silver Birch, the Red Maple, the Hackmatack, and the Jewish Book Award. A former psychologist, Kathy now travels the globe speaking to children and adults about the importance of keeping the memory of the Holocaust alive. Kathy lives in Toronto with her family.